TROUBLED WATERS

ROSEMARY HAYES

**Hodder
Children's
Books**

a division of Hodder Headline Limited

A Catalogue record for this book is available from
the British Library

ISBN 0 340 85469 3

Typeset in Bembo by Avon DataSet Ltd,
Bidford-on-Avon, Warwickshire

Printed and bound in Great Britain by
Bookmarque Ltd, Croydon, Surrey

The paper and board used in this paperback by
Hodder Children's Books are natural recyclable products
made from wood grown in sustainable forests.
The manufacturing processes conform to the environmental
regulations of the country of origin.

Hodder Children's Books
A Division of Hodder Headline Limited
338 Euston Road
London NW1 3BH

To Laura, with Love

Acknowledgements

I am very grateful to Scott Krieger for giving
me so much of his time and for explaining
about the work of The London Connection.

I acknowledge, as a source,
the following publications:

London Labour and the London Poor
by Henry Mayhew (Penguin)
The Victorian Underworld
by Donald Thomas (John Murray)
The Complete Servant
by Samuel and Sarah Adams (Southover Press)
The Victorian Town Child
by Pamela Horn (Sutton Publishing)

1

London, October 1835

'’Ere Abbie, stick that under yer skirts,' whispered Jim, handing her an apple.

Abbie stared at it. 'You never stole it, Jim?' she asked, anxiously.

'Nah!' Jim pointed in the direction of one of the fruit-sellers. 'He give it me for 'elping him.'

Carefully, Abbie tucked the apple under her torn skirt. She looked down at her feet and examined her new boots with pride. Well, they weren't exactly new; Mam had got them off the street clothes-seller. She'd been lucky. If you had a spare shilling, it was easy enough to buy second-hand clothes from the street sellers, but they didn't often have boots. You wore your boots until they fell apart, or you grew out of them. And then you passed them on down the family.

Abbie knelt down and polished her boots with the sleeve of her dress and, as she did, looked round the busy scene. People coming and going with horses

1

and carts, barrows being pushed along by the costermongers, or pulled by their donkeys, goods being unloaded and everyone shouting at the tops of their voices. The loudest of all was the hump-backed young man standing outside the public house with a basket of herrings and haddocks yelling, 'Yarmouth herrings – three a penny.'

It wasn't so bad helping out at Whitechapel Market in the summer, but now it was autumn and already there was a tang of cold in the air. A bitter wind came whipping up and caught at Abbie's thin clothes and tangled hair. She pulled her shawl more tightly round her shoulders and got up off her knees.

The market sprawled down each side of Whitechapel Road, noisy and colourful. She and Jim had helped out here since they were little.

She watched Jim as he strutted around on the other side of the road. Although he was twelve – two years older than her – he was small and skinny; but then so were most of the kids who swarmed round the market traders, sweeping the streets, running errands, all competing for a handout to keep them alive another day.

Jim was her only brother; the other brothers and sisters had died, some when they were babies, so she hardly remembered them, some when they were older. But it was a fact of life. No good dwelling on it. It was the same for everyone she knew. Everywhere in London there were sick children. And this winter, more would die.

The swirling fogs and the damp which came up from the Thames didn't help. Abbie shivered and thought of her dad. He worked as a waterman on the river, ferrying passengers across, but at this time of year trade was slack. And every winter his coughing got worse; sometimes the whole of the house where they lodged was filled with the harsh, shuddering noise of his cough.

Suddenly there was a commotion behind Abbie. She turned round quickly and saw a group of ragged urchins approaching her. She'd seen these boys often enough before and she was scared of them. They were barefoot, wild and desperate and she knew exactly what they were going to do. They would find an old lady or an old man, on their own by a stall, push them over and grab their money bowl.

Abbie dodged round a cart, out of their way, and crossed over to old Lil's stall. In the summer, Lil sold flowers but in winter time she made what she could from selling baskets of firewood and some cheap bits of jewellery.

'Watch out, Lil!' she called.

Lil looked up. Immediately, she understood. She emptied her money bowl into her pocket and huddled out of the way. Abbie, quick as a flash, sat herself on Lil's stool and picked up a tawdry necklace.

'Anyone wanta buy a loverly necklace,' she sang out, her eyes never leaving the gang of urchins.

The boys hardly gave her a glance. They'd seen her before and they knew she had a brother who worked the market. They wouldn't bother with the likes of her.

They passed on and Lil emerged.

'Thank you, my darling,' she puffed, straightening her skirts and her bonnet.

Together, Lil and Abbie watched as the boys progressed up the street.

'They'll not leave 'til they've picked a few pockets and emptied a few money bowls,' sighed Lil.

Abbie put her hand into Lil's. It was cold and knotted with arthritis. 'You shouldn't be out here, Lil,' she said.

Lil nodded. 'Aye. I'll not survive another winter, dearie,' she said. There was no self-pity in her voice. This was how it was. A fact of life.

Abbie looked upset. 'Can't you do some other work?'

Lil smiled. The wrinkled, weatherbeaten face under her bonnet was transformed for a moment and Abbie saw that once she must have been pretty. But her smile also revealed a row of rotting teeth.

'What else could I do?' said Lil.

'What about that relation of yours? The one with the rag-and-bone shop? Couldn't he help you?'

'Huh! He's a mean fellow, dear, he'd not help me. He makes a good living, though. He pays tuppence a

pound for the rags and sells them on at a tidy profit.'
Lil sniffed. 'But that shop of his stinks; I sleep there in
the winter and I tell you, Abbie, I'm that glad to get
out into the fresh air again.'

Abbie sighed. Lil was a market worker, born and
bred. For Lil it was market work, or starve – or die in
the poorhouse.

'And what about you, young Abbie? You'll not be
working in the market all yer life, I'll warrant!'

Abbie shook her head. 'I want to go into service, Lil,
if I can find a position in a respectable house.'

Lil sighed. 'Service, eh? Now that would be a fine
thing.'

Abbie nodded. 'Mam's teaching me to sew,' she said,
'and I go to the church school when I can to learn my
letters. Then, when I'm twelve, Mam'll try and find a
position for me.'

'And what of Jim? Does he get schooling, too?'

'Oh yes. Mam and Dad pays a penny a week for
both of us.' Abbie hesitated. 'But he doesn't go often.
He's not got much patience for learning his letters and
doing sums and that.'

They both glanced over to the far side of the road,
where Jim was bawling out at passers-by: 'Apples,
fine apples, ha'penny a lot! Come and buy the juicy
apples.'

Jim was in a good position. It was easy to catch the
customers where he stood, near to the man roasting

chestnuts. People walking up and down the road would stop and warm their hands at the brazier and buy chestnuts. And once they stopped, Jim would be there, smiling and holding out the fruit for them to see.

'You tell that boy to learn his letters, too,' said Lil. 'I never had no learning. Soon as I was old enough to walk, I was set to work. I often wished I'd 'ad some learning.'

Abbie smiled. 'Oh, Jim'll be fine, Lil. He's quick and he's got his eyes open. He makes everyone laugh and he's ever so popular. He'll always find a chance to earn an honest penny.'

The crowd of urchins had crossed to the other side of the street and were working their way along the stalls, but they didn't seem interested in causing trouble today.

Lil wasn't so sure. She pointed at them. 'They're waiting for something, you mark my words.'

Abbie frowned. They looked innocent enough, standing around, chatting. Were they really waiting for something?

Bedford, November, present day

Things must be bad if I'm writing a diary! But I've got to tell someone how I'm feeling, even if it's only a piece of paper! Is this sad, or what?

Today Mum said she was thinking of marrying Keith. I can't believe she'd do it; I hate him and so does Matt. And, worse than that, she actually asked me if I'd mind being called by Keith's surname! Becky Armitage instead of Becky Ford. This really upset me. I said no way! Just because Mum thinks she wants to marry him, that doesn't make him my dad. Nothing will ever make him my dad.

Thinking about Dad still makes me cry, even now. He was great. Everything was so much easier. It never mattered what I said then. And Matt worshipped Dad. They got on really well.

But that was when Matt was thirteen. I suppose they might have quarrelled now – now that Matt's sixteen. I tell you, brothers are such an unbelievable PAIN. One moment Matt's really friendly and the next he's all moody and just grunts at me.

Anyway, today – this evening – Matt and Keith were rowing again. I was lying upstairs on my bed with my headphones jammed over my ears, listening to the new CD Katie lent me, when there was all this shouting downstairs.

I tried not to listen, but Keith was really yelling at Matt. Not that it was about anything different. He was just banging on about Matt's school work, his attitude, his rudeness, his untidiness. Same old stuff. Nothing new.

But then he had a go about Matt's band. He told him it was a load of rubbish.

Bad move.

Matt really didn't like it when he laid into him about the band.

Matt's no brainbox and he's pretty lazy at schoolwork, but he and his friends have a really great band. Matt plays keyboard and composes most of the songs. And he's good. I mean really good. Sometimes when I've heard him (usually when I've sneaked up and listened to a band practice and they haven't known I'm there) I'm amazed that this is my smelly teenage brother! He's completely different when he's doing his music. I think he's really talented and I know it's the only thing he takes seriously. He knows exactly how he wants everything to sound, he's really organized about it and the others respect him.

And this evening Keith was telling him to give up the band and do some work for his GCSEs.

Matt exploded.

Mum tried to calm them down. Poor Mum. She's always trying to keep the peace between the two of them.

Matt pounded up the stairs and went into his bedroom, slamming the door behind him.

I don't usually poke my nose in, but somehow tonight's row sounded worse than usual. I went out on to the landing and hovered outside Matt's door for a bit. In the end, I went in. The room was a mess, as usual, with stuff all over the floor. Matt was lying on his bed and I could see he'd been crying.

At first, he just told me to piss off, but after a bit I started talking about his band and he opened up. He told me how he *needed this multi-track recorder to make a proper demo tape. He was desperate for it.*

While we were talking Matt put his hands on his knees and started to rock to and fro. It's funny; he always does that when he's upset.

Later on I went downstairs and talked to Mum on her own, while Keith was out walking the dog. I tried to persuade her to help Matt get the multi-track but she didn't want to know. And when I reminded her that Dad had played in a band once, she got quite cross with me.

It's all such a mess. I wish it was like it was before. Before Dad died.

London, October 1835

Out of the corner of her eye, Abbie watched the gang of urchins. She knew they wouldn't hurt her, but they still scared her.

Suddenly, as if from nowhere, an older man joined them. He was dark haired, with a straggling beard and greasy clothes. He spoke to the boys in a whisper, then turned and walked quickly back down the street.

Jim stepped right out into his path. 'Apples, sir. Lovely juicy apples. Come and buy them.'

The man stopped in his tracks, then he swore at Jim and knocked the apple he was holding out of his hand.

'Let me pass, damn you!'

Jim picked up the apple from the street and wiped it down on his jacket. Then he tossed it in the air.

'What a lovely *gentleman*,' he sang out. 'So polite, so charming!'

Everyone round the stall laughed.

The man turned back briefly and spat, then he melted away into the crowd.

'That's Greasy Will. He's setting something up,' muttered Lil, uneasily. 'You can depend on it.'

Abbie kept her eyes on Jim. Why couldn't he learn to keep his mouth shut? It didn't do to go making enemies of men like that greasy, shifty Will fellow.

' 'Ere we come!' said Lil, suddenly. 'A bunch of toffs. That's what they've bin waiting for.'

She was right. In the distance, a coach had stopped and coming down the Whitechapel Road were a group of finely dressed ladies and gentlemen, moving from one stall to the next, fingering the wares for sale, talking loudly to each other.

Abbie gazed at the dresses the women wore. Perhaps one day she'd be a ladies' maid in a grand house and she'd see dresses like that. Perhaps she'd get to look after them. She sighed and rubbed her hands together. She'd have liked to go over the road and warm her hands at the brazier, but she didn't want to leave Lil. With that group of urchins about and the rich toffs coming down the road, Lil might be right. There could be trouble brewing.

The grand ladies were heading for the fruit stall.

'Come and warm yourselves, ladies,' said Jim. ' 'Ave some tasty chestnuts and buy some fine juicy apples to take 'ome.'

Abbie watched him with pride. When he chose, Jim could charm the very birds off the trees. He had a quick wit and a ready smile.

Soon he was in conversation with the ladies, complimenting them on their gowns and remarking on the fine hats and canes of their gentlemen. It wasn't long before he'd made a sale and then, it seemed, all the toffs wanted to buy fruit from him.

Abbie nudged Lil. 'See, Jim'll be all right. He'll charm himself through life.'

Lil smiled. 'Well, I 'ope you're right my love. He's certainly got a way with him, that lad. He'll be a ladies' man when 'e grows up, you mark my words.'

The group of toffs moved off and Jim did a little dance behind their backs. He saw Abbie over the road and waved to her. She grinned and waved back.

Abbie looked round quickly to see if Greasy Will was still around, but he had vanished and so had the urchins. Abbie sighed with relief.

'They've gone, Lil. Those rough boys have gone.'

'Umm,' said Lil. 'An' what 'ave they taken along with them, I wonder?'

The party of toffs moved further down the street.

'Hope they stop 'ere on their way back to their

carriage,' said Lil, watching their progress.

Soon, the ladies and gentlemen turned round and started walking slowly back the way they'd come.

'They want to be back in front of their fine parlour fires for their tea,' said Lil, bitterly, blowing on her cold hands.

Abbie straightened her hair, wiped her hands down her dress and got up off the stool. She stood in front of Lil's stall and bobbed a curtsy as the first lady approached.

'A fine necklace for you, ma'am,' she said, holding out one of Lil's trinkets.

The woman smiled at her and walked on. Abbie sighed. She knew she'd not sell anything to them. They weren't interested in cheap jewellery or baskets of firewood.

As the group walked past, one of the gentlemen was saying it was time they went back to the carriage or they'd be late. He put his hand in his waistcoat pocket but then he stopped and frowned. He rummaged in the pocket again.

'What the deuce?' he exclaimed. 'Where's my pocket-watch?'

Another gentleman came up to him. 'What is it, Frobisher?'

'My gold watch,' he shouted. 'It's gone! I've been robbed!'

The ladies gasped and looked round nervously.

'This place is full of pickpockets,' said the other gentleman. 'I fear you'll never find the thief.'

But the gentleman called Frobisher had gone very red in the face.

'That watch was a gift from my father, God rest his soul. It means a lot to me and, by God, I'll get it back.'

'Steady, Frobisher,' said the other, trying to calm him.

But Frobisher was shouting now. 'If anyone saw anything, you're to tell me, d'you hear! You won't be able to sell it, you know, you'll get nothing for it. There's an inscription on the back. No hawker will touch it.'

He paused, then raised his voice again.

'A guinea to the man who can tell me where it is!'

There was a gasp round the market. A guinea! A guinea was more than many stallholders would take in a month!

'Well?' shouted Frobisher. 'Will anyone come forward?'

Suddenly, in front of Abbie, someone was pushing through the gentry. Abbie drew back, disgusted.

It was Greasy Will. He had his cap in his hands and he was twisting it this way and that.

He stood in front of Frobisher.

'Begging yer pardon, sir.'

'Yes?'

'A word in your ear, if you please, sir.'

13

Frobisher frowned with distaste, but bent forward to listen as Greasy Will whispered in his ear.

Frobisher stood up. 'Are you sure of this, man?'

Greasy Will nodded solemnly.

Frobisher turned to one of the other gentlemen. 'Quick, call a constable.'

'What's going on?' asked Abbie.

' 'E's asking for one of them new-fangled bobbies,' said Lil.

'Whatever for? If one of those urchins has gone off with the gentleman's watch, the bobby will never find it.'

Lil shrugged. 'You can be sure Greasy Will thinks he's going to get his guinea, some way or another.'

The stallholders went back to work. No one wanted trouble.

The group of ladies and gentlemen stood around uneasily and then all of them, except Frobisher and one other gentleman, began to walk back towards their carriage. A few minutes later, two bobbies arrived, wearing their hard hats and swinging their truncheons. Greasy Will and Frobisher spoke to them.

And then, with an amazing turn of speed, the bobbies moved.

It was so sudden and unexpected that it took Abbie a few moments to realize what they were doing.

The two bobbies strode over to Jim, closely followed by Greasy Will and Frobisher.

'That's him,' said Greasy Will, pointing at Jim. 'That's the dirty thieving urchin wot took your watch, sir. When he was admiring of your hat and your cane, sir, and telling the ladies 'ow beautiful they looked. When you were off your guard, sir, that's when he took it.'

'Where is it, you filthy little sneak? Where's my watch?' boomed Frobisher, poking Jim in the chest.

Jim was so surprised that he dropped the apple he was holding. For a moment his good humour deserted him.

'What are you talking about? What's going on?'

'Oh, he's playing the innocent is he,' sneered Greasy Will.

Jim looked so genuinely astounded that, for a moment, Frobisher hesitated. 'Are you *sure* this was the boy?'

'Oh, don't you be took in by all that charm, sir,' said Greasy Will. 'I saw him take your watch and I saw him hand it over to one of his little mates who run off with it. I would've said something there and then, but I was scared those rough lads would tear me limb from limb.'

One of the bobbies put a hand on Jim's shoulder. 'Is this true, boy?'

Jim angrily shook off the big hand.

'No! No, of course it's not true!'

Greasy Will laughed. ' 'Course he *would* say that, wouldn't he, sir? So why don't yer search his pockets for 'im. Yer won't find the gentleman's watch, 'cos I saw wot 'e did with that, but I warrant you'll find plenty of other stolen trinkets.'

The two bobbies loomed over Jim. One pinned his arms behind him while the other searched him.

'That's it,' said Greasy Will, rubbing his hands together with glee. 'Look in the jacket pocket. That's the deep one where he'll have stashed it away.'

The constable drew out a fine linen handkerchief from Jim's jacket pocket.

'There,' said Will. 'What did I tell you?'

'By God, man, you're right,' exclaimed Frobisher. 'That's my handkerchief!'

'And no doubt there's more,' said Will, calmly.

The constable dug deep into Jim's jacket pocket.

'Does this belong to you, sir?'

He was holding up a fine piece of lace.

Frobisher exploded with wrath. 'That's my wife's,' he shouted. 'How dare you, you common little . . . little vermin!'

Abbie was looking on in horror. Jim seemed to be struck dumb. She ran across the road to him, slipping once on a slimy piece of discarded fruit and falling headfirst into the muck. But she felt no pain. She leapt up and went to his side.

'He's not a thief,' she shouted at the constable, her chest heaving.

Jim suddenly came to life.

'I didn't take anything,' he said shakily.

'Of course he didn't,' said Abbie. 'It must have been planted on him. That Greasy Will must have planted it on him.'

'Out of the way, girl,' said Frobisher, pushing her so that she fell down again. Then he turned to the constables. 'I don't think we need more proof, do we? He was beside us, distracting us with his chatter, urging us to buy apples and chestnuts. He was close to us for several minutes. Quite long enough for a light-fingered piece of scum like him to do his work.'

Then, with a sneer of distaste, Frobisher handed a guinea to Greasy Will.

'I didn't take anything,' repeated Jim.

Abbie pulled herself up from the ground and stood beside him.

'That's the man you want,' she shouted, pointing at Greasy Will. 'He's the thief. Him and his gang of urchins.'

Greasy Will cracked his knuckles and rubbed his guinea between his palms.

'I seen what I seen,' he said.

Frobisher looked up the street to where the carriage was waiting. He reached for his watch again, realized it wasn't there and then crossly straightened his shoulders, adjusted his hat and began to walk off.

'Take him away, constable, if you please.'

'Come on, you!' said the one of the bobbies. The other put handcuffs on Jim's wrists.

'Where are you taking him?' whispered Abbie, trying to hold back the tears.

The man shrugged. 'We'll take him to the station for now, then I shouldn't wonder if he'll be having a little stay in prison.'

Abbie went very pale. She'd heard about what went on in prison. Everyone in the market had stories to tell about the wretched folk who ended up in prison.

She touched Jim's arm. 'We'll soon have you free,' she said.

Jim looked at her, full in the face. 'I never took a thing, Abbie.'

'I know,' she said gently.

'Tell our mam that I never stole a thing.'

Abbie nodded. She could feel the tears pricking her eyes; she didn't dare speak.

'Come on. Stop wasting time,' said one of the constables. Then, one burly man on either side, they marched Jim up the street, round the corner and out of sight.

Bedford, November, present day

Today's a day I'll never forget. Not for the rest of my life.
It was a relief to be back at school after last weekend.

Most of the rows happen at the weekend. During the week, Keith comes home late and Matt and I don't see so much of him.

Matt was in quite a good mood (for him) when we set off for school. He was in one of those 'Let's tease the kid sister' moods. I don't mind. He can be really good fun sometimes. We were laughing and fooling about as we turned the corner and went into the road that leads to the school.

Then we stopped and stared. There were a couple of police cars at the school entrance.

We were still fooling about but we started to walk more quickly, to find out what was happening.

There was a crowd of kids hanging around, being dramatic about it all, whispering and nudging. Honestly, there are so many drama queens at our school!

Apparently there had been a break-in and some school equipment had been taken. So what? I thought. No big deal then. No one's murdered a teacher or anything.

We all hung around for a bit longer but nothing was happening so we went to our classrooms, with some of the kids stilling oo-ing and ah-ing about it. Then, a bit later, we were all called to a special Assembly in the main hall and the headteacher told us what had happened.

It seemed that there wasn't much damage but some equipment had been stolen, including the school's new digital multi-track recorder.

At first I didn't take it in; I wasn't really listening. But then it hit me. The multi-track recorder had gone!

It was then that I had this ghastly sick feeling. I turned round to look at Matt. He was standing very still, staring at the headteacher.

I knew *he* wouldn't have taken it. He wouldn't be such an idiot.

Then I tried to remember what he was doing last night. He'd gone out. He'd gone to visit his friend Jake. I relaxed then. He couldn't have done it. He was with Jake.

I didn't see him until after school, but when I did, I knew something was wrong.

He told me he'd lied. He hadn't been at Jake's at all. He'd just gone for a walk to clear his head but he thought Mum would give him a hard time if he told her he just wanted to get out of the house, so he'd lied to her and said he was going over to Jake's.

As we came into our street, we saw the police cars again, two of them, pulled up outside our house.

I don't think I've ever felt so scared. Mum and Keith met us at the door. Keith was the last person we wanted to see. Mum must have called him at work and asked him to come home.

The police were calm and polite, but they were persistent. Poor Matt stumbled over his words, stammered and even shouted. They wouldn't let me in the room but I listened at the door. He was saying all the wrong things to them and getting muddled and upset.

The police interviewed Mum and Keith separately. I wanted to tell them that I knew it wasn't Matt. It couldn't be him.

Even if he did want the equipment, he'd never steal it. He wouldn't be such a fool. But they didn't want to talk to me.

Then, after the police had gone, Keith went right off the wall. He was like a madman, ranting and raving and yelling at Matt.

But for once Matt didn't shout back. He just kept repeating that he hadn't done anything wrong.

One time, I thought that Keith was going to hit Matt. But Mum put herself between them.

Eventually, Keith finished shouting and we had tea. It was horrible. No one said much. Matt said nothing at all and hardly touched his food. Mum looked as if she'd been crying.

After tea, I went to my bedroom. I said I had a lot of homework but I didn't even open a book. I just stared at the posters on my wall.

I'm really worried. What's going to happen to Matt? If Mum and Keith don't believe him, then who will?

Next day...

I slept badly last night. I had scary dreams about burglars and once I woke up with a jerk, sure that someone was in my room.

If only, when I'd had that feeling, I'd switched on the light. Perhaps I could have stopped him. Perhaps things would be different now.

Then, this morning, when I woke up properly, I saw it.

A scrawled note, lying on my desk.

I scrambled out of bed, rubbing my eyes, but even before I read the words, I knew what they'd say.

'I didn't take the stuff, Becky, I swear. I know this looks bad but I just can't stand being here any more. Matt.'

London, October 1835

Abbie started to run after the constables, but she felt a hand on her arm.

'They'll take him to the lock-up just round the corner, love,' said Lil. 'There's nothing you can do on yer own. Best run home now and tell your ma and pa.'

Abbie stared at her. 'He wouldn't steal anything,' she whispered.

Lil gave her a hug. 'I know, my darling, but you'll have the devil's own job proving it.'

Then she gave Abbie a little shove. 'Go on home, Abbie. Hurry now.'

Abbie ran as fast as she could, but it was a long way from the Whitechapel Road down to the river. She raced down to the Aldgate, then the Minories and at last into Tower Hill.

She could run no longer. Her sides ached and her legs were leaden. She slowed to a walk, clutching her stomach. She stared up at the great Tower of London and a huge sob caught in her throat. She thought of all the prisoners who had perished in the Tower in years gone by. Then she thought of Jim.

He couldn't go to prison – could he?

She stumbled on. Her father's boat was moored at Tower Steps and their lodgings weren't far away, dwarfed by the great Tower.

She paused for a moment outside their lodgings. What would she say? How would she tell them? Her mam and pa were hardworking people. They'd never been in any trouble.

At last she could put it off no longer. With a heavy heart, she pushed open the door.

Her mother was by the window upstairs, her head bent over her sewing, working as fast as she could while the light lasted.

She looked up when Abbie came in and was opening her mouth to say a cheerful greeting to her when the words died on her lips. Instead, she jumped to her feet, scattering pins and material about her. She came to Abbie and took her hands.

'Whatever is it, girl? You look that pale. What ails you?'

'It's Jim!' she blurted out.

'What's happened?'

'They've taken him.'

Mam shook her. 'Who? Who's taken him?'

'The constables – the bobbies. They've taken him away. He's been accused of stealing, Mam.'

23

2

London, October 1835

Mam still had hold of her shoulders. Abbie could feel her grip tightening. Then Mam let go and dropped down to her knees, wringing her hands.

'How could he, Abbie? How could he disgrace us like this?'

'Mam, he didn't steal *anything*! It was a plant. That Greasy Will planted stuff on him.'

But Mam wasn't listening. She shook her head. 'He's a wild one, that boy. I've always said so.'

'*Mam*, Jim didn't take anything,' repeated Abbie.

Mam looked at her then. 'You don't know that, Abbie, and even if you're right, girl, how'd folks like us ever prove it?'

'I don't know, Mam,' said Abbie, helplessly, 'but we must try!'

Mam shook her head. 'It's hopeless,' she whispered.

Abbie stamped her foot. 'No!' she shouted.

Mam looked up and sighed. For a long moment

they just stared at each other. 'Very well, girl,' said Mam, at last, quietly. 'Have it yer own way, but it won't do a bit of good, you mark my words. Go and fetch your pa, then, and we'll all go and pay a visit to the lock-up.'

Abbie didn't waste any time. She was out of the door in a second, running down to the river; but when she reached Tower Steps, she hesitated. She'd not often been there on her own, certainly not this late in the day. Usually, she and Jim went together. She choked back the tears and went to the very edge of the wide river.

It was getting dark and the tide was going out, so her pa must have tied up his boat by now. The gas lights were being lit, one by one, alongside the riverbank, but they just made the shadows bigger and more threatening. The mud oozed, black and fetid, near her feet and she thought pityingly of the mudlarks, further down the river; children of her age, and younger, who scavenged near the coal wharves, knee-deep in mud, looking for something – anything – that they could sell so they could keep food in their bellies.

She looked around her but the shadows and the wisps of fog made it difficult to see. There were a lot of people milling about, but she couldn't make out their faces.

'Pa!' she called out, nervously, but there was no reply.

Then a shape loomed up out of the darkness and someone put a hand on her shoulder. She jumped and thought immediately of the tales her pa had told her, tales of drownings, of river pirates and smugglers.

'It's little Abbie, ain't it?'

Wide-eyed, Abbie looked up into the face of a huge man. Then she relaxed. It was one of her pa's mates. Another waterman.

'What are you doing down here on yer own, Abbie? Where's that rascal of a brother of yours?'

Abbie was glad that the man couldn't see her face. She sniffed and wiped her eyes with the back of her hand.

'Please sir,' she said. 'I've come to fetch my pa. Can you find him for me?'

The man looked down at her. 'Come along then, girl, we don't want you taking cold by this damp old river. We'll go and seek him out.'

When they found him, Pa was deep in conversation with another man. Abbie could see immediately that he was a cut above the watermen; he was probably a vegetable grower from upriver, one of them who owned a market garden. Pa didn't look pleased to see Abbie.

'Best wait 'til he's finished off his business,' whispered Pa's mate to Abbie. 'It wouldn't do to interrupt a deal now, would it?'

Abbie shook her head. She supposed her pa was arranging to ferry fruit and vegetables down the river next season. She knew he'd been trying to get in on this trade for a long time. She waited, desperate with impatience.

Pa's mate walked away. 'I've got to go, Abbie. But yer'll be safe now yer've found yer pa.'

Abbie nodded into the darkness. 'Thank you,' she whispered faintly.

Pa took no notice of Abbie as she stood, hugging herself in the cold, a few metres away from him. His conversation with the other man didn't seem to be going too well. The grower (if that's who he was) raised his voice several times and though Pa never shouted back, he kept having coughing spasms, which seemed to madden the other man. At last, the stranger spun round and elbowed his way through the crowd, muttering angrily as he went.

Pa seemed distracted. Abbie crept up to him and tugged at his sleeve.

'Pa, you must come with me,' she whispered urgently.

'What are you doing here, girl?' he asked crossly. 'You know I've told you not to come here on your own. It's no place for a young girl, especially at night. Where's Jim?'

'It's because of Jim I'm here,' said Abbie. Then, suddenly, she couldn't stop the tears. 'They've taken him, Pa. He's in the lock-up,' she sobbed.

She had his full attention then. Telling her to hush up, he put his arm round her and propelled her away from the river's edge. When they were clear of the crowd, he stopped.

'What happened? Quick, girl, tell me everything!'

Between sobs, she repeated her story.

'Oh sweet Lord,' whispered Pa. 'The young fool!'

Then he subsided into another coughing fit. But as soon as it was over, he took Abbie's hand.

'Come on then, girl, we'll get your mother and we'll go and see where he is.'

Mam was already outside the door, wearing her shawl and bonnet, and, without a word, the three of them hurried back up to Whitechapel Road.

Abbie stuck close to her mam and pa. The lamps were all lit now and she knew very well that more thieving gangs would be out and about. It was much easier to steal – from stalls or from passers-by – under cover of darkness.

Mam and Pa had no thought for the thieves; they were set on finding Jim. It was only Abbie who glanced round fearfully at the groups of ragged urchins standing on street corners. Some of them had boot-blacking-boxes slung on their backs by a leather belt, some were crouching in groups on the pavement. Once she saw a couple of them scampering along beside a hansom cab, nimbly turning somersaults and catching coins from the passengers.

Abbie and her parents walked the length of Whitechapel Road. Some of the stallholders had left (there was no sign of Lil) but new ones had come, bringing fresh supplies on their carts or barrows. There was noise and shouting and bustle as they pushed their way up the street.

'Lil said they'd take him to the lock-up round the corner,' panted Abbie, as they came towards the end of the market.

'Aye,' said Pa, grimly. 'That'll be the one in Mile End Road. We're nearly there.'

Abbie looked up at him. Even in the dark, she could see the sweat pouring from his face. She knew the running and pushing and shoving made him ill. His breathing was noisy and came in short gasps. He began to cough again and they had to stop.

Mam put a hand on Pa's arm. 'You're not well,' she said gently.

'I'm well enough to find my son,' said Pa, shortly, 'Come on.'

It was less crowded in Mile End Road. Pa seemed to know where the lock-up was and headed purposefully along the cobbled road. At a pair of dingy doors, he hesitated.

'This is it,' he said, turning to Mam. 'You and Abbie stay here outside.'

Mam said nothing, but she took Abbie's hand and followed Pa inside the building. He looked back and frowned at them, but he didn't send them away.

Once inside the police station, Abbie realized

how shabby she and her parents looked. Pa removed his cap and, between spasms of coughing, enquired about Jim.

With agonizing slowness, the bobby moved his grimy finger down a list. At last, he grunted.

'Taken in Whitechapel Road this afternoon,' he read. 'For stealing a valuable gold pocket-watch belonging to James Frobisher Esquire and linen and lace also belonging to said gentleman.'

'He didn't do it,' blurted out Abbie. 'He was set up by Greasy Will!'

But the bobby didn't even glance at her.

Instead, he addressed Pa. ' 'E's 'ere all right.'

'He never took it,' burst out Abbie again. 'It was a plant.' She twisted her dress in her hands. 'Oh please, sir, there's been a mistake.'

Pa glared at her.

The bobby folded his arms and said nothing.

Gently, Mam pushed Abbie away and bobbed a curtsy. 'Please, sir, can we see him?'

The bobby hesitated. He looked at Mam's face, tense and white with anxiety, stray hair matted across it. For a moment he said nothing, then he sighed and reached behind him for a bunch of keys.

'Come with me,' he said.

They followed him down some stairs to the lock-up cells. It was badly lit and Abbie stumbled once and nearly lost her footing.

At the sound of footsteps, there was a general movement from inside the cells. People came to the barred doors and shouted. Some stuck their hands between the bars.

Abbie glanced up at one of the doors – and then wished she had kept her eyes on the floor in front of her. A drunken man with greasy matted hair and a filthy beard spat from between the bars and the globule of spittle landed on her boots. He screamed with laughter and some of his cell-mates joined in.

They stopped at the last cell at the end of the corridor. The bobby held up his list to the feeble light of the gas lamp.

'In 'ere,' he said.

They couldn't see anything because the light was so bad.

'Jim 'Arris?' shouted the bobby.

There was a shuffling from inside the cell.

'That you, Jim?' said a voice. 'Yer wanted.'

Then Jim's voice. 'I'm Jim Harris.'

The sound of his voice turned Abbie's stomach upside down. He sounded so scared. This wasn't her brother – her cheeky, can't-touch-me, know-it-all brother.

'Jim?' said Pa.

The bobby turned to Pa. 'Yer'll 'ave to talk to him through the bars. I can't open the door. I'm on my own and if I turn the key they'd all rush out like so many sewer rats.'

Pa nodded. Then he went close up to the door and peered through the bars.

'Jim?'

Suddenly, Jim's face appeared at the bars, set into the top of the door. He was too small to reach up and see through them but he'd been hoisted up by a couple of other lads.

As soon as she saw his face, Mam burst into tears. His eyes were huge and scared and his face was scratched and bleeding.

'I didn't do it, Mam. I swear!' Then he saw Abbie. 'Tell them, Abbie,' he said desperately. 'I didn't do it!'

There was raucous laughter behind him.

'I didn't do it, Mam,' mimicked some of the others. 'I swear I didn't do it.'

'I believe you, son,' said Mam, softly. So softly that Abbie was sure Jim hadn't heard.

'We know you didn't,' said Abbie, trying not to cry. 'It was that foul man, Greasy Will. He planted the stuff on you.'

Jim's face disappeared from view and they heard him land heavily on the cell floor. His cell-mates had dropped him, tiring of holding him up at the bars.

'Didn't do it! Didn't do it! No one listens to you 'ere, yer mad urchin,' said one of the lads. They all laughed at that.

Pa looked at Mam and Abbie. 'They're right,' he said. 'Who's going ter listen to a rough lad like him, the son of a common Thames waterman?'

Abbie wanted to scream and shout, but what good would it do? If she made a fuss here, she'd as like find herself locked up for affray or some other offence.

Wearily, they followed the bobby up the stone stairs again. Abbie pulled at Mam's arm.

'What will happen to him?' she whispered.

But Mam just shook her head.

Back upstairs, Abbie bravely repeated her question, this time to the bobby. He looked down at her quite kindly.

'We don't keep 'em 'ere, lass. In the morning he'll be moved off to one of the prisons before 'e goes to court.'

'Where? Which prison?'

The bobby shrugged. 'Newgate, Millbank. Depends.'

Mam clutched at Abbie's hand.

'Oh, please sir,' she begged. 'Can we not stop this?'

'Hush woman,' said Pa. He had seen the expression on the bobby's face.

'The law will take its course,' said the bobby, who was losing patience. He slammed shut the book on the table in front of him and frowned.

'There's nothing different about your lad, *madam*! 'E's just like the rest of 'em. 'E was taken fair and square, in possession of stolen property. So don't go expecting any sympathy from the law.'

Before Abbie could open her mouth again, Pa had mumbled good evening, replaced his cap and was pulling her and Mam towards the door, shoving them in front of him. As soon as they were out on the dark street, Abbie exploded.

'It's so unfair!' she shouted. 'Jim didn't do it!'

'Hush,' said Pa, looking back at the police station. 'There's nothing we can do.'

Mam looked desperate. 'How will we manage?' she muttered. 'Jim always came home with a few pennies. We'll be sorely tried without his money.'

Abbie swallowed. It was as if Mam knew that Jim would be found guilty. Found guilty and then sentenced for who knew how long for something he'd not done.

'He may get off, Mam,' said Abbie.

But Mam said nothing. Neither did Pa.

They were glad to turn back into Whitechapel Road. They were dead weary by now and they walked slowly with their heads bowed, but there was some comfort in the hustle and bustle of the market, still in full swing.

The pieman had come to the market and was doing a brisk trade, his pie-can on his arm.

'Pies all 'ot! Eel, beef or mutton pies! Penny pies, all 'ot, all 'ot!'

Abbie's mouth watered as she caught a whiff of the pies. A pieman was a rare sight in London now that the pie shops were all the rage.

The cake-men were out, too, their trays slung round their necks – and there was a coffee stall on the corner, surrounded by customers. But Abbie and her family hurried on. They had no money to spend on such luxuries.

Mam looked up once, seeing a costermonger she knew. He greeted her with a cheery wave and she smiled wanly back.

'They make a good living, the costers,' she said, sighing. 'At least ten shillings a week – and sometimes more.'

'Aye,' said Pa. 'But you have to be born a coster. They're a rough lot and they don't take kindly to outsiders.' He had another spasm of coughing and they all stood still until it was over.

Mam looked at him, her face full of concern.

'It's no good looking at me that way, woman, and thinking I can change,' he said at last. 'I'm a waterman, born and bred. It's the only life I understand.'

Mam nodded into the darkness. And sewing's the only skill I have,' she said, 'but I'm lucky if I get more than four shillings for a whole week's work.'

Abbie felt helpless. 'Maybe I could be a costergirl,' she said. 'I could give up my schooling and work full-time in the market.'

Mam rounded on her. 'Don't talk such nonsense, girl! You keep at your letters, do you hear? Then maybe we'll get you a position in a respectable house. At least, that way, you'll always have a roof over your head and food in your belly.'

The next week dragged past. Abbie went several times to the market, to help on Lil's stall, but she couldn't join in with the jostling and shouting and selling of wares. She had no stomach for it.

Once, she caught a glimpse of Greasy Will. In a fury, she ran after him. Lil screamed at her to come back but Abbie heard nothing and saw nothing except Jim's scared face at the cell bars.

She sprinted on, yelling, accusing him of framing Jim. She had nearly caught him up, when suddenly she felt herself grabbed from behind by a pair of strong arms.

'Le me go! Let me get at him!' she screamed, kicking and struggling.

'No, I'll not let you go, you young vixen,' said a man's voice, laughing.

Abbie screwed her head round to look at her captor. It was Mam's friend, the costermonger they'd seen the other evening.

'He had a knife, lass,' said the man, quietly. 'And I don't doubt he'd have used it to slit your pretty throat.'

He let her go then and she dropped to the ground, winded.

The man helped her up. 'Thank you,' she whispered. Then, to her dismay, she started to cry like a baby.

'Hush, lass,' said the man, kindly. 'There are more ways than one to kill a cat.'

Abbie stared at him. 'What d'you mean?'

The man put his finger on the side of his nose and stared into the distance. 'I doubt he'll be working the market again,' he said. 'Sneaking on an innocent boy hasn't won him any friends and we costers have ways of dealing with the likes of him.'

Abbie shivered. She didn't want to hear what they had planned for Greasy Will, though she thought it unlikely they'd catch him. He'd disappear at the smell of any trouble.

'What of Jim?' she asked. 'Can you help him? Can you speak for 'im and say 'e didn't do nothing?'

The man sniffed and wiped his nose on the back of his hand. 'The costers and those damn bobbies are sworn enemies, Abbie, you know that. They'd never take no notice of the likes of us.'

He looked down at her anxious face. 'But we'll find out where's Jim's gone, lass. I can't say more than that.'

Bedford, December, present day

It's a month since Matt disappeared and we haven't heard a thing. The atmosphere in this place is unreal. Mum's desperate; she's not sleeping properly and I know she can't face Christmas without Matt. I often hear her prowling about the house at night. Things are bad between her and Keith. She can't forgive him for what he's done. She blames him for driving Matt away – and she's right. She doesn't say much, she doesn't shout at him or anything, but she just ignores him. And when he goes to put his arm round her, she shrugs him away.

Keith's changed, too. At first he ranted and raved, saying Matt was a thief and a coward, but when he said those things, Mum just stared at him and you could see how angry she was. He knew he was to blame, and he just blustered on. But Mum's silent fury has got to him now. He's started smoking again and he spends even more time out of the house, down the pub or walking the dog. He knows he's blown it with Mum. There's no talk of wedding bells now, thank God, and the atmosphere here is terrible.

Mum looks ill. She won't talk about Matt with Keith – she doesn't talk to him much at all – but she does to me. And she cries all the time.

The morning after Matt left I found his mobile on his bed. That's when I knew it wasn't just some stupid gesture.

He'd meant to go and he doesn't want to be found.

It's not as if we haven't tried to find him. The police have tried and so has Mum. She's been in touch with Missing Persons, with the Salvation Army, you name it, she's tried it. But there's been nothing; not even a tiny clue.

If only he'd just phone to say he's OK.

Part of me feels sorry for Matt but another part of me feels really angry with him. How dare he leave us like this? He's broken Mum's heart and he's left me to cope with everything. Sometimes I think, even if we do find him, I'll never forgive him for all the trouble he's caused.

It's been really bad for me at school, too. Everyone thinks he did the break-in and took the stuff. Even Katie, my so-called best friend.

I never thought I could fall out with Katie. We've been best friends since primary school. But she said it was obvious Matt did it. How dare she!

We had a huge row and I don't speak to her now. I don't speak to many people. Having your brother called a thief isn't any fun.

A week later . . .

Today, something good happened at last!

When I came home from school, a policeman was just leaving our house. 'That's good?' I hear you say! Well, of course, that was what I thought. More bad news. Something terrible must have happened to Matt. My stomach tightened up and I stood where I was, trying not to cry.

I didn't want to talk to the policeman, so I waited until

he'd driven off and then I ran up the street, my heart pounding.

But when I got in, Mum was crying, but she was smiling, too. She hugged me and told me that they'd found the person who broke into the school!

I couldn't believe it!

Apparently, some of the stuff was offered to a man who runs a market stall miles away. The stallholder took it but then he got scared and contacted the police. Anyway, the guy selling it was caught on closed-circuit camera. He lives round here and he's got a record.

So it looks as though Matt's in the clear.

But how can we tell him? I'm sure he's gone to London. He often used to talk about all the music going on in London. But even if he is there, we'll never find him. So he'll go on thinking that the police are looking for him.

London, November 1835

The winter set in early, with biting winds and thick fog.

And Jim had been taken to Millbank Prison, a huge, grim place further down the river, where he was waiting to learn his fate.

Things weren't easy for Abbie's family. The trade for waterman was very slow and, in any case, Pa's cough was that bad he could hardly handle the boat sometimes. Mam worked all the daylight hours at her sewing and Abbie picked up what work she could, running errands and helping at the market. She tried to help Mam with the sewing, but she was still too clumsy and slow.

Abbie worried about her Pa – and she worried about old Lil, too. Sometimes, Lil was too sick to come to the market and Abbie would go round to visit her at the rag-and-bone shop, where she lay in a heap in a corner, hardly any different from the other heaps nearby, of coloured or white rags. The smell was dreadful, but Abbie didn't mind. She was used to bad smells.

'How can I earn some more pennies, Lil?' said Abbie, one day.

Lil laughed. Her whole body shook and her face creased up.

'Look at me, girl,' she said. 'A heap of rags and bones like the rest of the stuff here! And you're asking me how to earn pennies!' She shifted beneath her rags. 'Lor, child, if I knew that, d'you think I'd be killing myself at that stall and sleeping in this filthy place?'

'But there must be something!' said Abbie, desperately.

Lil scratched herself. 'Trouble is, dearie, they all stick together. The crossing sweepers have their patches, the street sellers and buyers and specially the costers. They all have their stamping grounds and woe betide you if you try and step on their patch.'

Abbie moved closer to Lil, for warmth.

'Why don't the costers get on with the police, Lil?' she said suddenly.

Lil sniffed. 'I dunno, but there's no love lost there. The costers have to get a licence from the police, then the police make them move on from place to place. I reckon they're jealous that the costers make a good living from their trade.'

Abbie began to scratch, too. She was no stranger to fleas and lice, but the heaps of rags were infested. They almost moved on their own. To distract herself, she tried to think of all the jobs she'd seen people do in the streets.

'P'raps I could collect the *pure* Lil? There's always a mass of dog dung on the streets.'

Lil shook her head. 'Nah, you don't want to do that filthy, stinking job, Abbie. Though they make a few pence, the pure collectors. But it's no job for a young girl.'

'What do they do with the pure, once they've got it?'

'Sell it to the tanneries, dear. They rub it on the animal skins to cure them.'

Lil sat up, slowly and painfully.

'Anyways, girl, look on the bright side; maybe that brother of yours'll be earning again soon.'

Abbie shook her head. 'I don't think so, Lil. Greasy Will disappeared once he heard that the costers were after him. The costers may speak up for Jim, but the police never trust the costers, so no good will come of it. He'll serve time in prison, you can depend on it.'

'Well, 'e's not been in trouble before. They won't give him a long sentence.'

Abbie couldn't bear to think of Jim in prison. She'd never seen Millbank, but she'd heard stories. She got up and walked to the door.

I'd better be off, Lil, or Mam will start fretting.'

Abbie came home to the familiar scene of her mam straining her eyes, sewing by candlelight while her pa sat in the corner, coughing and wheezing.

She emptied the few pennies she'd earned into her pa's lap.

'Sorry it's not more,' she said.

Pa patted her head. 'You're a champion lass, Abbie,' he said. 'We couldn't keep any food on the table without you and your ma slaving away every minute God sends.'

Later that evening, as they were eating their meal of bread and some thin gruel, Pa said, 'I'm going to take the skiff down the river to Millbank tomorrow on the early tide.'

Mam's spoon clattered onto the floor. 'You're never going to see Jim?' she whispered.

Pa nodded. 'It's good way down the river, but I can manage it.'

Abbie stared at him. 'Can I come with you, Pa?'

Pa looked across at Ma. 'What do you reckon?'

Ma nodded. 'She could help with the boat, if you were took bad,' she said quietly.

'Aye, she could that,' said Pa, shortly.

The next morning, Abbie and Pa set off at first light. Abbie wore all the clothes she possessed, but she still shivered in the dank, cold morning air as she helped Pa push the boat off.

Pa rowed steadily down the main channel in the middle of the river. As yet, there was not much traffic and they journeyed in eerie silence, except for the slap-slap of the oars on the water and the cry of water birds.

The weak, watery winter sun was a little higher in the sky when the grim walls of Millbank Prison came into view.

'It's huge, Pa! I never thought it to be so big!'

Pa nodded grimly. For a moment, he shipped his oars and they stared together at the long, highwalls, with towers evenly spaced at intervals, which stretched for such a distance along the riverbank.

'Poor Jim,' whispered Abbie.

Pa sighed. 'Come on then, lass, we'd better face up to it,' he said.

They rowed to the bank and Pa spoke to other watermen who were tied up there. At first they were hostile to an intruder – a waterman from another 'patch' – but he explained his reasons for being there and they were soon friendly enough.

'They're a good bunch, the watermen,' said Pa. 'As long as you don't trespass on another's trade, they'll look after their own.'

It took several hours to get inside the prison and to be granted leave to see Jim, but at last the turnkey led them through long stone corridors and to the huge cell where crowds of men – the young with the old – were sitting or lying or standing listlessly. Some shouted and screamed, some huddled on the floor.

Abbie grabbed Pa's arm.

'He's there, Pa. There in the corner!'

For a moment, Pa lost his stern expression and his face crumpled. Then, fiercely, he drew his fist across his eyes and cleared his throat.

'Jim!' he called. 'Jim Harris.'

The boy huddled in the corner looked up listlessly.

'Jim,' Pa called again.

Jim got up and looked around him in confusion. Then he saw Pa and Abbie at the bars which separated the prisoners from the corridor.

Slowly, his head bowed, he shambled towards them.

'He looks so small,' gasped Abbie. 'And Pa, they've shackled his legs!'

'Hush, lass. Be brave. Don't let him see you take on so.'

Jim pushed his way to the front of the cell. He held on to the bars and peered through them at Pa and Abbie.

When Abbie looked at him more closely, she saw that although he was pale, he looked well nourished. At least he was getting some food in here; probably more than she was.

'How are you, boy?' said Pa, his voice breaking.

Jim looked him in the eyes and there was, for a moment, a flash of his old spirit. He didn't answer Pa's question.

'I never took nothing, Pa,' he said.

'I know, son. I know.'

'What's happening?' asked Abbie. 'When's your trial?'

'Trial!' Jim spat on to the floor. 'I've had my trial.'

Abbie put her hands over Jim's and gripped them.

'Some trial,' said Jim. 'They had that toff Frobisher in court and the judge believed him and believed the bobby wot took me.'

'And the costers?' asked Abbie. 'Did they speak up for you?'

'They tried,' said Jim. 'But they didn't help my case none. They swore at the bobbies and the judge turned them out of the court.'

'So . . . ?' Abbie couldn't finish.

'So. I'm convicted of theft. Convicted for six years for something I never did.'

Pa looked shattered. 'Six years,' he muttered. 'Six years! There's no justice in that!'

'And will you stay here at Millbank?' whispered Abbie, when she found her voice.

Jim looked down at the stone floor.

'No,' he said, shortly.

'Then where . . . ?'

'They're sending me to the colonies,' said Jim.

'No!' shouted Pa, and immediately began a painful bout of coughing.

Jim hung his head and waited until the spasm had passed.

'It could be worse, I suppose,' he said. He grinned suddenly. 'They say it's sunny over there.'

'Where?' asked Abbie. 'Where are you going.'

'Van Diemen's Land,' said Jim. 'I'm going to a prison for boys on Tasman Island.'

Abbie stared at Pa. 'Where's Van Diemen's Land?'

Pa shook his head.

'They say it'll be months at sea,' said Jim. 'That's all I know.'

Abbie felt numb. 'Jim!' she whispered.

'It's a new prison,' said Jim, speaking slowly. 'Only been running a year or two. It's for boys from twelve to eighteen.'

'What's it called, this place?' asked Pa, at last.

'Point Puer,' said Jim. 'They call it Point Puer.'

3

London, June 1837

It was a warm day and Abbie was walking along the river's edge, feeling the sun on her face. She was growing up. She was quick with her needle now, and neat. Mam was that pleased with how she'd come on.

She stopped at the place where she and Pa had left that grey November morning, to go down to Millbank to see Jim. She stared out across the water.

The river looked friendly now. The sun shone on the water and there were rowing boats and sailing boats and big steamers all jostling for position. Just coming into view were some skiffs laden with fruit and vegetables for the markets, coming downriver from the growers in Woolwich. Abbie shaded her eyes to see them more clearly.

Pa had managed to do a deal with one of the growers and last summer he'd earned more than usual, so they'd not been so hard put to it to find food and money for the rent. But then the winter had come and his coughing had got that bad you knew it was agony for him.

Mam and Abbie had watched him struggle to control the spasms, but they'd got worse and worse.

'Don't go out on the river today,' Mam had begged him, over and over again.

But he took no notice.

Then one morning last December some of his watermen friends had found him, lying motionless at the bottom of the skiff, drifting down the river. The river which was so much a part of his life had reclaimed him in death.

Abbie sighed. She and Mam were on their own now. They knew nothing of Jim; they didn't know whether they'd ever hear from him again.

And they couldn't survive another winter on what they earned now. The time had come for Abbie to try to find a position in a household. It was a risk; the daughter of a waterman and a needlewoman wasn't the sort they usually took. They preferred girls whose families had been in service themselves.

But Mam was determined that Abbie should try and get on in life. She knew the value of a warm bed and regular food in the belly. She had given her some pennies she'd saved and Abbie had put this with what she'd managed to save herself and gone down to Petticoat Lane, where she'd spent the morning picking over clothes from the street sellers.

Other people, seeing what she'd bought, wouldn't think she'd done that well. There were tears in the dress, the bonnet had half the edging ripped off and the petticoat had no drawstrings. But Abbie knew that she and Mam could make them good as new. And she'd even found some boots; they were scuffed and down at heel, but if they blacked them up, you'd not notice.

She must look her best for their visit to Hatton Garden.

Mam mended linen for a Mrs Payne. Mrs Payne was the housekeeper for a big house up in the West End. She'd been a good friend to Mam over the years, putting all the work she could her way. Mam had spoken to her about finding Abbie a position, but Mrs Payne said there was no position at the place where she worked. But she'd given them some advice and told Mam where to go to see about a job for Abbie.

The London Society for the Encouragement of Faithful Female Servants, in Hatton Garden.

'She says it's free to register, Abbie, and it's been going a long while. It's the best place to start.'

'It sounds too grand for the likes of us,' said Abbie, nervously.

Mam frowned and bit her lip. 'We've got to get you settled before long,' she said. 'You know that. We can't keep going as we are. And I'm sure if you look clean and answer up well, they'll look kindly on you.'

'What shall I say if they ask about the family?' said Abbie. 'We've never been in service.' She hesitated. 'And what about Jim? What shall I say about him?'

Mam shook her head.

'I don't like you to lie, Abbie, but just for once, you'll have to. They won't want the sister of a thief.'

She saw Abbie was going to protest. 'It's no good, girl. He's been transported, so he's marked. Whatever we say folks won't believe he's innocent; best say he's a sailor,' she went on. 'And it's no good pretending we've ever been in service, either,' she added. 'You'll just have to say you want to better yourself.'

When Abbie got home, Mam ran an expert eye over the clothes. She was pleased with what she saw.

'They'll do well, girl.'

While they set to to mend Abbie's new clothes, Mam said, 'They say all the big houses are on the lookout for help, what with the young queen's coronation coming up and all the balls and parties and that.'

The young Queen Victoria would be crowned very soon.

Abbie smiled. 'Only eighteen!' she said in wonder. 'And a whole country to rule!'

Mam smiled, too. 'Aye, she's that young. But she's got the country behind her.'

It was true. Everyone in London was talking of the coronation and of the young Queen Victoria. In the market, Abbie had heard that there'd be a grand procession to Westminster Abbey, with all the carriages and horses and soldiers. And with all the excitement and all the visitors and the comings and goings, there should be a lot of extra work around for a young servant girl.

The next day, Mam and Abbie were up early to walk to the Society's place in Hatton Garden. It was a long way; at first they kept to the river, past London Bridge and Southwark, and then at Blackfriars Bridge they turned up towards the City.

It was another hot day and Abbie was perspiring in her new clothes. As they entered Shoe Lane they saw a street trader selling ginger beer and lemonade. Mam stopped.

'I've got a few pennies with me,' she said, looking at Abbie's hot face.

Abbie smiled. This was a rare treat.

'Two glasses of ginger beer, if you please,' said Mam, handing over two halfpennies to the man behind the cart.

They stood close together, drinking their ginger beer slowly. They didn't know this part of London and they were nervous.

Mam asked the beer-seller if they were right for Hatton Garden and he nodded and pointed up the street. 'Straight on, my lovelies, over Holborn Circus and then you're there,' he said.

When they reached the Society, the woman behind the large table looked so stern that Abbie's nerve nearly failed her.

She wore a high-necked blouse with a cameo brooch at her throat and she had a little elegant watch pinned at her bosom. Her hair was swept up at the sides and she was frowning.

'Can you read and write?'

Abbie bobbed a curtsy. 'Yes, ma'am,' she whispered, 'I learnt my letters at the church school.' She wondered how well she was supposed to read and write. She only formed her letters very slowly and she couldn't read anything but the simplest words.

'Speak up, girl!'

'Yes, ma'am,' she repeated. She could feel her knees trembling, partly from all the walking and partly from fear.

'And what else?'

'If you please, I can sew a neat seam, ma'am,' said Abbie.

'Who taught you?'

'My mother, ma'am.' Abbie hesitated. 'She takes in linen to mend.'

The woman noticed Mam for the first time, standing in a corner, with her hands together and her eyes downcast.

At last the woman behind the table looked a bit more friendly.

'Is it you who was recommended by Mrs Payne?'

Mam stepped forward and bobbed. 'Yes, ma'am.' Then, shyly, she took out a sheet of paper from her purse.

'Mrs Payne said to give you this, ma'am,' she said.

'Oh? What does it say?'

Mam blushed. 'I can't read it, ma'am, but I believe it says that she's always been pleased with my work.'

The woman read it and then handed it back to Mam. She turned to Abbie.

'And are you as hard-working and faithful as your mother?'

Abbie looked at her steadily. 'Yes, ma'am,' she whispered.

The woman grunted. Then she started firing questions at Abbie. They went on and on. Abbie tried hard to answer honestly and not be frightened, but it was difficult. Then came the one she'd been dreading.

'And what of the rest of your family?'

Abbie swallowed. 'My pa died last winter,' she whispered. 'He was a Thames waterman.' She hesitated. 'And my brother Jim is a sailor.' She hesitated again. 'The others all died little.'

The woman grunted. She looked Abbie up and down several times and then wrote some details in a special book. Then she rang a bell and another woman appeared with a large ledger which she handed over.

The first woman ran her finger down the list and

then the finger stopped, hovering over a name and address.

'Yes,' she muttered to herself. 'Yes, this may suit.'

She drew a sheet of blank paper towards her and started to write again.

Abbie and Mam watched in silence. They didn't dare interrupt her.

At last she had finished.

'Take my letter to this address,' she said. 'And, if you are lucky enough to be taken on for work, don't let me down. The reputation of the Society is very high among the good families of this city. Be sure not to disgrace it.'

'Thank you, ma'am,' said Abbie. And then she added, nervously, 'If you please, what is the position?'

The woman looked at her sternly. 'The household needs an under housemaid,' she said. 'It is a big house and a busy household. If you are offered the position, you can consider yourself lucky, especially as no one in your family has been in service before.'

'Yes ma'am, thank you ma'am,' said Abbie.

'Read the address at the top,' said the woman.

Abbie took the paper and, with her finger moving along the letters, she spelt out C-A-V-E-N-D-I-S-H followed by S-Q-U-A-R-E.

'And what does that say?'

'Does it say "Cavendish Square"?' stammered Abbie.

The woman nodded. 'That is the house of a fine,

noble family,' she said. 'If they take to you, it will be a good position and if you do your work diligently and are quiet and polite, you may, in time, be able to work your way up to being an upper housemaid. Who knows.'

The woman consulted the watch pinned to her blouse.

'I strongly advise you to go there at once,' she said. 'There may be other young girls being considered for this position.'

Mam had no idea where Cavendish Square was, but the woman gave them directions, and they set off, clutching the letter from the Society.

Outside in the street, Mam hugged Abbie.

'Oh Mam, I'm frightened,' said Abbie. 'It's that quick. Couldn't we go to the grand house another day?'

Mam looked nervous, too. 'We'd best do as she says,' she said. 'And we're nearer to it here. I 'ope you've got the way into your head, girl. It was all a muddle to me and I didn't like to ask again.'

'Down Holborn,' repeated Abbie. 'Round St Giles, then on up to Regent Street. Turn up there.'

They trudged for nearly an hour; no crossing sweepers cleared the streets for them when they needed to cross. The sweepers knew they'd get no pennies from the likes of Abbie and her mam. They lifted their skirts from the horse manure and other filth, but even so, the dust swirled up and over them whenever a horse-drawn cab clattered by on the cobbled streets.

They missed their way a few times and had to ask passers-by, so when they at last reached the house in Cavendish Square, they were both covered in dust and grime.

Mam spat on her kerchief and dabbed at Abbie's face and brushed at her skirt with her hands.

Abbie straightened her cap and wiped her sweaty hands on Mam's kerchief.

They stared at the big black door at the top of whitened front steps. The brass knocker gleamed and flashed in the sun.

Abbie turned and looked at the square itself. It was so beautiful and peaceful, with its rich green trees and tended gardens. She'd never seen anything so grand. Mam was ill at ease.

'We'd best find the servants' door,' she muttered.

They made their way round to the mews at the back and found the tradesmen's entrance.

Mam knocked on the door.

While they waited, a groom and a fine-looking bay horse entered the mews, the horse's hooves clattering on the cobbles. Abbie watched as the groom dismounted and led the horse into one of the stables behind her.

Then the back door to the house was opened by a maidservant, dressed neatly in a long black skirt, a blouse, a cap and a pinafore.

'Yes?' she asked.

Mam cleared her throat. 'Please, miss,' she said. 'We've come to see the housekeeper, Mrs Plum. It's about the position of under housemaid.'

The girl looked unsure.

Mam drew out the paper from the Society.

'We have a letter,' she said.

'Wait 'ere please,' said the girl. Then she shut the door and disappeared.

Mam and Abbie looked at each other. Abbie turned again to look at the horses behind her. She could see four loose boxes and a coach house. How grand it was.

After a couple of minutes, the girl came back.

'Follow me, if you please,' she said.

She led them along a back passage, past a huge kitchen, with gleaming pots and pans and a shiny blackened range, to a small parlour.

It was a neat, well-appointed room with a fireplace, two chairs with antimacassars on their backs, a big potted plant and a round table covered with a green tasselled cloth. By the window, which looked into the side street, stood a tall woman.

The housekeeper, Mrs Plum.

She came towards them and Abbie bobbed a curtsy. Mam did the same.

They gave Mrs Plum the letter and explained that they had come direct from the Society.

Mrs Plum glanced at the letter briefly, then she

walked up to Abbie and put her hand under her chin.

'Are you a hard worker, child?'

'Yes ma'am,' whispered Abbie.

'And she's a clean child,' added Mam, hastily, 'All the walking's made us dusty.'

Mrs Plum smiled. 'You must be out on your feet,' she said kindly. Then she went to the parlour door. 'Sarah,' she shouted, 'Bring some lemonade, please.'

For the first time, Abbie dared to look properly at Mrs Plum. At first she'd thought her terrifying, but when she'd smiled at them, Abbie felt better. Her face was creased into laughter lines, so she must smile often. Perhaps she was not so frightening after all.

The maid came in with three glasses of lemonade on a tray with a crocheted cloth on it. She put the tray carefully on the table.

'Will that be all, Mrs Plum?'

'Yes Sarah. All for now, thank you.'

As they drank their lemonade, Mrs Plum asked Abbie many of the same questions that the Society lady had asked. Again, she answered them all truthfully except about Jim.

Then Mrs Plum told her the duties of the under housemaid.

'Cleaning and scouring the stoves and grates, scouring the coal scuttles, kettles and fire-irons, beating and cleaning the carpets, scouring the floors, stairs and passages, washing the dishes when there is company.'

Mrs Plum took a sip of her lemonade.

'It's good that you are a needlewoman, Abbie,' she said. 'For in the afternoons you can be put to mending the bed linen and the table linen and stockings and suchlike.'

She paused and looked at Abbie. Abbie looked down at her hands.

'I'm a hard worker, ma'am. I'll do my best.'

Mrs Plum smiled and patted her hand. 'Of course, you'll have to keep your own linen in good order, too. Oh – and sometimes you'll be needed to help make the beds and carry up the coals and water.'

Mrs Plum cleared her throat and took another sip of lemonade.

'Do you think you can learn to do all that?'

Abbie nodded. She looked at Mam.

'She's a good girl, Mrs Plum,' said Mam. 'I know she'll do her best.'

After that, everything was a bit of a blur for Abbie. Before she could take it all in, it had been decided.

She would start as an under maid at the house in Cavendish Square next Monday.

Her wages would be £12 per year, paid half-yearly.

Bedford, June, present day

I've not written in this for ages; didn't have the heart, somehow.

There's been no news about Matt. Not a word and Mum really has tried everything. As the days go by and nothing happens, she gets more depressed. As well as blaming Keith, she blames herself. She thinks she should have stood up for Matt more.

I think she's forgotten what a pain he could be. I know I shouldn't say that now he's missing, but, to be honest, he wasn't the easiest . . .

Mum's got really thin. She was always dieting before, but now she doesn't need to. She's too thin. And she's not eating properly. Sometimes it feels as if I'm the mother and she's the child. I'm always going on at her, nagging her to eat properly. Talk about role reversal!

Then, yesterday, the weirdest thing happened!

We were on this school trip to London and we'd been to the Science Museum. It was a hot day and we were all sticky and fed up with traipsing round taking notes for our coursework. Mrs Lane, our Science teacher, was being a pain – well, she's always a pain. She practically jumps up and down with excitement at things bubbling in test tubes and boring old bits of machinery whirring away.

The only good thing about the museum was the static electricity. Me and Katie kept rubbing this balloon thing and making our hair stand on end. Katie looked really scary! Mrs boring Lane made us stop and dragged us off to look at some other bit of stuff that was whirring or clicking or chugging or flashing or something.

Anyway, it was on the way back that it happened.

We were walking down to the tube station, chatting and giggling, when I noticed this guy sitting in the corner.

He had a notice propped up beside him, 'No job, no food'.

He muttered something as we walked by, but we took no notice. You see kids like him a lot in London. I just went on talking to Katie, making her laugh with take-offs of Mrs Lane.

So I've no idea what made me turn and look back at the guy again, but I did. And I looked at him properly this time. He was so young – not much older than me – and he sat there, with no hope, in this desperate heap.

Then, suddenly, I knew what had made me look back. My stomach turned over. There was something familiar about him! He was holding his knees and rocking, backwards and forwards, again and again, just like Matt used to do when he was upset.

I stood still and stared at him and my brain seemed to freeze. It couldn't possibly be him – could it? Everything around me faded into the background. I couldn't hear Katie's chatter any more, I didn't see the crowds hurrying towards the platform. All I could hear was the drumming in my brain and I could only see this guy, huddled there, rocking to and fro, with his head bowed.

I stood completely still, being jostled by everyone else. Katie tugged at my sleeve.

'Come on, Becky.'

I didn't hear her. My heart was racing and I began to sob. I twisted away from her and forced myself back to the boy.

Katie followed me. 'Becky, what the hell . . . ?'

'It's Matt!'

But my voice was choking and the sound was lost.

I reached him at last and knelt down beside him.

'Matt?'

The boy kept his head bowed.

He didn't know me.

Of course he didn't.

It wasn't Matt after all. It was just a guy who looked a bit like him.

I gave him everything I had in my purse. It wasn't much. Then I made Katie empty out her purse, too. We dropped it all into his lap.

Katie was frantic. 'Come on, Becky, we'll lose the others.'

I turned to go with her, sobbing, feeling desperate. Why did I feel so guilty?

'Where will you sleep tonight?' I asked the boy.

He looked up at me then, surprised. The first expression I'd seen in his blank face.

He mumbled something. It sounded like 'hostel'.

'Which hostel?'

He muttered something, but I didn't catch it. And Katie was pulling at my arm.

I had to go then. The rest of our party was already round the next corner and Katie and I weren't sure where we were going. We sprinted to catch them up, pushing past people who got in our way.

Katie was great on the way home. We're friends again now.

When they found the person who broke into the school, she was really sorry she'd said it was Matt. It took a long time, but now we're friends like we were before Matt left. Well, almost, anyway.

On the way home, all I wanted to do was cry. I've never felt so miserable.

What if Matt is like that? What if he's huddled in a corner of a stinking underground station, begging?

Katie just squeezed my hand.

'I can't bear to think of him like that, Katie,' I'd said.

'But what can you do? The police have looked for him. Your mum's tried everything.'

I don't know why, but suddenly I knew exactly what I would do.

'I'm going to try and find him myself.'

She didn't say anything. She thought it was just because I was upset.

She thinks I'll forget the boy in the tube station. But I won't.

As I went to bed last night, I kept thinking of him.

What hostel was he at? How did he get there? What happens to homeless kids in London? Does anyone look out for them?

Matt was always talking about London – about all the music opportunities being there. I'm more sure than ever that Matt went to London. It's not far to go and it's so easy to lose yourself in a big city.

London, September 1837

Abbie had settled in well at Cavendish Square. She learned quickly and she soon got into the routine of the household.

She liked Sarah, the other under maid, straight away, and they became good friends, giggling and gossiping together.

'When I first came, I thought you were that smart, in your uniform. I was scared of you,' said Abbie.

'*You*, scared of *me*?' said Sarah.

Abbie nodded. 'I was scared of everything. It was all so different.'

Sarah sometimes moaned about the work, but Abbie never ceased to be grateful. She knew what it meant to go hungry. And she knew what it meant to be cold. At least here she always had good food and she was never cold.

It was a large household and, below stairs, the butler, Mr Hodges, and the housekeeper, Mrs Plum, ruled the servants. But no one was unkind to Abbie, even the upper housemaid, Agnes, who was in charge of Abbie and Sarah. Sometimes, when there was company staying and lots going on – dinner parties, picnics and the like – Abbie felt exhausted as she clambered up the stairs to the little attic bedroom she shared with Sarah. But then, everyone worked hard at these times.

There were lots of other servants besides Abbie, Sarah, Agnes, Mrs Plum and Mr Hodges. There was a cook, a lady's maid, a young ladies' maid, a nurse, a laundry maid, a kitchen maid, a nursery maid, a coachman, two grooms, a valet and a gardener.

There was also a governness, Miss Beecham, but Abbie had little to do with her, or, for that matter, with the gentry. Lord and Lady Fanshaw had six children. There were two girls – Miss Eleanor and Miss Florrie. Miss Eleanor was thirteen (like Abbie) and Miss Florrie a year younger. Then there were three younger children – a boy and two more girls – who were mostly in the nursery, except when they came downstairs to be taken for walks or when they came into the drawing room to be presented to visitors or to spend a little time with their parents.

Abbie hardly ever saw Miss Eleanor or Miss Florrie. They had a lady's maid of their own and they spent their time in the schoolroom, or riding out with the groom, or visiting with their parents or the governess. Mostly, she and Sarah were downstairs, scrubbing the passages and cleaning and scouring in the kitchen, or helping with the washing of the dishes.

Occasionally, they'd been set to scour the grates in the gentry's bedrooms upstairs, or haul coal and water there. When she'd seen the fine linen and ornaments in these rooms, Abbie had marvelled.

She thought often of old Lil's tawdry trinkets in the market. Nothing like that would be found in a grand house like this!

In the summer, there had been such a flurry and excitement around the young Queen Victoria's coronation. Picnics, dinners, parties, relatives come up to stay from the country. Abbie had run up and down the stairs and passages, doing double the work she was normally set. But she didn't mind. She was caught up in the excitement and the gossip, and sometimes caught a glimpse of some of the beautiful dresses and cloaks worn by Lady Fanshaw and Miss Eleanor and Miss Florrie.

After their midday dinner, Sarah and Abbie were set to making and mending the household linen with Agnes, the upper housemaid. It was soon evident that Abbie was more skilful with her needle than either of the others.

One day, as they were sitting in Mrs Plum's parlour, their heads bent over their work, Agnes said, 'Abbie, the young ladies' maid has noticed your work. She's asked if you'd be able to alter some of Miss Florrie's frocks for her; she's growing apace and it seems a crying shame to pay an outside dressmaker to make all the alterations.'

So Abbie began to do simple alterations to the young ladies' dresses and bonnets and suchlike.

'Do you help them try on the dresses, Abbie?' asked

Sarah, as they were getting into bed one night. Abbie nodded. 'I have to, Sarah. How else would I know where to put the pins and how much to let out or take in!'

Sarah sighed and looked down at her plain shift. 'All those pretty things. Wouldn't it be grand if we could wear them, too!'

'Don't be soft,' said Abbie. 'The likes of us'll never wear such finery.'

'But we can dream,' said Sarah.

Abbie laughed. 'You're always dreaming, Sarah!'

Sarah struggled out of her shift and stared out of the tiny window at the night sky.

'Did you hear that the cook's leaving us, Abbie?'

Abbie nodded. 'Yes, Agnes told me. She's off to live with her sister in the country.'

'Hope the new cook's as good as her.'

'And as good to us,' agreed Abbie. They were sometimes slipped titbits or asked to sample a spoon of something when Mrs Plum wasn't around.

But the new cook wasn't as friendly.

Mrs Flanders was certainly good at her job, but she had no time for lowly under housemaids.

'I don't like her,' said Sarah, one day. 'She makes me nervous.'

Abbie agreed. 'She makes me feel clumsy when I'm washing the dishes.'

'She's got an evil eye,' said Sarah.

Abbie giggled. 'Oh you don't 'alf go on, Sarah. An evil eye. What stuff and nonsense.'

But the atmosphere below stairs was less relaxed with Mrs Flanders ruling the kitchen.

Abbie had one half-day off every fortnight. She always went home to see her mam, usually setting off after her morning chores to make the long walk down to Tower Bridge. The previous cook had always given her some victuals to take home with her, enough to feed her and Mam for their dinner, but Abbie was frightened to ask for anything from Mrs Flanders.

'I'm that sorry, Mam,' she said, the first time she went home after Mrs Flanders was in charge. 'I daren't ask her for anything, she's such a fierce-looking woman.'

Mam smiled. 'I don't expect you to bring me food, girl. Though it was good while it lasted.'

Abbie, as always, chatted away about what had been happening in the household. And Mam wanted to know every detail.

'I'm so proud of you, girl. You've really come up in the world.'

Sometimes, they talked of Jim, but as time went by, they mentioned him less and less.

Bedford, July, present day

I'm still determined to try to find Matt myself and I keep thinking of how — where to start. Where haven't we looked? Who haven't we asked?

If only we just knew he was safe.

I can't stop thinking about that guy at the tube station. He keeps getting into my brain. At school, at home, even when I'm doing something fun. Katie and I were at a friend's birthday party the other day and right in the middle, when we were all listening to this really great music, there he was, pushing his way into my head.

Until I saw him, I'd sort of left Matt somewhere out there in limbo. I knew we'd done all we could to find him and I knew if I kept thinking about him all the time it would do my head in.

I had to get on with living my own life and seeing my friends. Matt was just a dull sadness and I'd only think of him when I saw his friends or heard a certain sort of music. Or sometimes, passing his bedroom door and remembering that dreadful night before he ran away.

But seeing that boy, rocking to and fro, just like Matt used to, that brought it all back. I feel really bad for forgetting Matt, and now I keep seeing him in my head, desperate and smelly, huddled in a doorway somewhere, begging.

I've not said anything to Mum about this. Well, there's no point. It would only upset her. She's probably already imagined all the bad things that could possibly have happened to Matt.

She doesn't talk about him much now – even to me. I guess because it upsets her so much and, like me, she's trying hard to get on with her own life.

I know, deep down, she'll never give up on him and I'm sure she thinks about him all the time. But the fight's gone out of her and she doesn't seem to have any energy. She doesn't know what else she can do to try and find Matt. At first, there were a few supposed 'sightings' of him and each time we'd get our hopes up. But the trail has gone completely cold now. He's yesterday's news and everyone has forgotten about him.

The trouble is, if he doesn't want to come home, no one can force him. He's over sixteen and the law says he's an adult and can do what he wants – even if it means he's breaking Mum's heart.

She's got really scrawny now and she's on all these pills. Pills to make her sleep and pills to stop her depression. She never used to be like this. She was always smiley and fun – and interested in everything. Now, she slops around the place like a zombie.

She tries hard to be interested in what I'm doing, but I can see it's an effort when she asks me about school or about parties and stuff. It used to be natural. Now it's forced. And she's scared for me. I can see it in her eyes. Scared that something awful might happen to me, too.

And as for Keith – I don't know why he hangs around. It's obvious Mum doesn't want him here but I suppose she can't stand the thought of a row.

I hate being in the house when Keith's there. The atmosphere's dreadful. I go out as much as I can, but then I feel guilty for leaving Mum.

Ever since I saw the guy at the tube, I've been thinking of other ways to try and find Matt. I'm sure there must be something I can do. But where to start? I keep tossing ideas round and round in my head, but come up with nothing; well, nothing we haven't tried already.

Then, this morning, I collected the newspaper from off the doormat and I was just glancing at it when something caught my eye.

There was an article in it about a place called The London Connection which helps homeless people in London.

I sat down on the stairs and read it, several times. There was a phone number, so I scribbled it down on the back of my hand.

I'll get in touch with them. I'll try to go and see them and find out what happens to homeless kids when they arrive in London.

At least it's something – somewhere to start. The summer holidays are coming up and I'm going to look for Matt myself. I still have this feeling that he's lost himself in London.

I had to get to school – I was already late – so it was break-time before I could make the phone call.

It took ages to get through to The London Connection, but, when I did, the bloke there was really helpful. I tried to explain what it was all about – about Matt running away and about how worried we were. But I knew I needed longer to explain and I wanted to speak to someone face to face.

'Can I come and see you?' I blurted out.

'Sure,' he said, calmly. 'Phone again and arrange a time to come, and someone will talk to you.'

I ran to my class then and arrived flushed and breathless. Katie nudged me and asked what I'd been doing.

I told her I'd tell her later.

When we'd finished the lesson, I told her. She's going to come with me to London.

I feel a bit better now; at least I'll be doing something, even if it leads nowhere.

But I won't tell Mum.

4

London, Winter 1841

Abbie was sixteen – nearly seventeen. Life in Cavendish Square had its ups and downs, but, on the whole, she was content.

It was her half-day, and she ran out of the back door into the mews.

'Morning, Jethro,' she called to the head groom, who was going into a loose box with some harness.

Jethro had been there for years. He'd been a good friend to Abbie, but she'd noticed how he'd changed over the past months. His back was bent with arthritis and his movements were slow and painful.

'Morning yerself, young Abbie,' he shouted back.

She paused at the half-door of the loose box and stroked the nose of the carriage horse inside.

' 'Eard the news, Abbie?'

'What news?'

'They're getting me another groom at last,' said Jethro.

'That's good. You need some more help.'

'Aye. A young man by the name of Edward. His uncle's a harness-maker, so he should know sommat about the work.'

'That's good news,' said Abbie, absently. 'But I'd best be on my way. It's a long walk to the Tower.'

'Off to see your mam?'

Abbie nodded.

'You're a good girl, Abbie 'Arris.'

Abbie ran round to the square. The crossing sweeper got up from where he'd been sitting on the ground and sprang to sweep away the horse droppings from the path across. Abbie fished in her purse and gave him a penny. He doffed his cap to her.

He'd been there for years, too. It was his 'patch', and a very good one, too. The gentry tipped him well – sixpence or sometimes more. Much more than Abbie could ever afford to give him. Before Mrs Flanders had taken over as cook, he used to be given food from the back door of the house, too.

But Mrs Flanders had put a stop to all that.

'Huh!' she'd said, when Abbie had suggested she take some leftovers to him. 'He makes a better living than you do and he hardly lifts a finger. I'll keep those leftovers here if you *don't* mind and turn them into soup.'

Mrs Flanders' temper hadn't improved over the years, but she was a very good cook even though most of the other servants were scared of her. And she was sweetness and light when it came to discussing the food with Lady Fanshaw. But Lady Fanshaw never saw the other side of her. The servants all had to mind their ps and qs with Mrs Flanders around.

Agnes had left and Abbie was now the upper housemaid. At first, she'd protested, saying that Sarah had been there longer, but Sarah urged her to take it on.

'You'd be better than me, Abbie, you know you would. And anyways,' she'd added, 'I don't want to tell folk what to do.'

So another under housemaid had been appointed to help Sarah.

Abbie found herself doing less of the scrubbing and polishing and more and more needlework.

'Anyone can scrub and polish, Abbie,' said Mrs Plum. 'But there's few can sew so neatly.'

Abbie lifted up her skirts and walked quickly in the direction of the river. She knew many of the street people along the way and waved and smiled at them. But she didn't stop to talk. She had little enough time with her mam as it was.

Abbie had become a very pretty girl. More than once, a man whistled at her or passed a remark at her face and figure. Once, some street entertainers, with a crowd watching them tumble and juggle, shouted out at her. But Abbie, though she blushed furiously, took no notice.

At last she arrived at Mam's lodgings. She'd kept the same lodgings even though Abbie gave her most of her earnings and she could have afforded better.

'I'm 'appy 'ere, girl. I know the place – and the folk roundabout. And it's close to the Thames, too.'

The Thames reminded her of Pa. Mam still walked down to the river sometimes and watched the watermen at work.

Abbie ran up the rickety steps to the door.

'Mam!'

Then Mam was at the door and giving her a hug. Abbie looked at her face.

'Mam, sommat's up. What is it?'

'Come in, girl, and close the door to keep out that wind.'

'What's wrong, Mam? Sommat's up, I know it is!'

'For heaven's sake, girl, will you sit down and take off your bonnet.'

Abbie did as she was told.

'*Now* will you tell me?' she said.

For answer, Mam thrust a letter at Abbie.

'It only came yesterday, Abbie.'

Frowning, Abbie turned it over in her hands. Her mam never had letters.

'Open it for me, girl!'

The envelope was flimsy and covered with grime.

'It looks as if it's come a fair way,' said Abbie, her heart beginning to race.

Abbie and her mam looked at each other. They were both thinking the same.

'It couldn't be from Jim, could it?' whispered Mam.

'Who else would write from foreign parts?' said Abbie.

'For God's sake open it then,' repeated Mam.

Abbie's hands were trembling, but she found a knife and carefully slit open the envelope. Then she drew out a sheet of flimsy paper, with neat writing on it. Quickly, she looked at the signature on the bottom.

'It *is* from Jim!' she shouted.

Mam nodded. 'I knew it. I've bin telling myself ever since it came yesterday. I knew it'd be from him.'

Abbie's heart was racing so fast that at first she couldn't make any sense of the writing. Then she took a deep breath and forced herself to read it slowly.

'It's well written,' said Abbie. 'He's learnt to write proper. He could never form his letters like this before.'

'But what does it *say* girl!' cried Mam, twisting her hands together in agitation.

Abbie looked at her mam and her eyes filled with tears.

'What's happened? Is he sick? Has he got into more trouble?' whispered Mam.

Abbie wiped her eyes. 'He's coming home, Mam! Jim's coming home!'

'He's never!' Mam grabbed Abbie round her waist and hugged her tightly.

They held each other, laughing together.

'I can't believe it. After all this time! He's really coming home!'

'But when, Abbie? When's he coming?'

Abbie looked at the letter again. 'It was written months ago,' she said. 'And it says, "I'll be back before Christmas". Nothing else. Just that he's in good health, that he thinks often of us and that he'll be home before Christmas.'

'Could be any time, then!'

Abbie nodded. She couldn't speak for the tears welling up inside her again.

'Oh Mam, it will be good to see him.'

'Won't it though? Won't it just?'

When Abbie got back to Cavendish Square that evening, she couldn't wait to tell Sarah the news, but she had to contain herself until they were alone in their attic bedroom.

'But you never spoke of him before,' said Sarah, confused. 'I didn't even know you 'ad a brother.'

Abbie blushed. She'd found it easier not to mention him than concoct some story about her sailor brother.

'Listen, Sarah, can you keep a secret?'

Sarah nodded, wide-eyed.

'When he was twelve, Jim was accused of stealing a watch.'

Sarah stared. Stealing! The brother of good, quiet, reliable Abbie?

'But he didn't do it, Sarah. It was a plant. Jim was innocent.'

'Then, what . . . ?'

'He didn't get a fair hearing, Sarah. And he was transported. He was sent to the colonies.'

Sarah sat down heavily on the edge of her bed. 'And 'e's coming 'ome now?'

Abbie nodded.

'That ain't 'alf romantic,' sighed Sarah. 'Back from foreign parts. I wonder what he'll be like?'

Abbie wondered, too. But aloud, she said, crossly, 'He'll just be Jim, like he always was, I expect.'

But would he just be the Jim she'd always known? Would he be changed from the light-hearted, cheeky lad she remembered? He'd be eighteen now, going on nineteen. What had he seen over there? What things had happened to him? She couldn't even begin to imagine it. Would they have anything to say to each other? What would he think of her life now, so settled here in a part of London he'd never entered? Would he think she'd forgotten her lowly beginnings? Would he blame her for bettering herself?

She couldn't sleep that night, tossing and turning in

her little bed while Sarah snored beside her.

At last she crept out of bed and looked out of the attic window on to the mews below. She stayed there a long time, thinking.

Long enough to see the night carts come down the mews to empty the buckets of night soil from the houses, and then trundle on their way.

The next day she was thoughtful and, after dinner was over, she went out into the mews for a few minutes before going up to start on the needlework.

No one seemed to be around the horses, so she talked softly to her favourite carriage horse and gave him a piece of apple she'd saved for him from her dinner.

Suddenly, there was a cough behind her.

' 'Scuse me, miss.'

Abbie spun round, embarrassed to be caught talking to the horse.

A young man holding a pitchfork stood there, also looking embarrassed. She'd not seen him before.

'Sorry, miss, but Mr Jethro says I gotta muck out Beau's box now.'

Abbie smiled and moved out of his way.

'You must be the new groom,' she said.

'Yes, miss. I'm Edward. Edward Roberts.'

'When did you start, Edward?'

'Yesterday, miss.'

The poor boy was blushing furiously and Abbie felt quite sorry for him.

'Well, good luck, Edward.'

'Thank you, miss.'

'I'm only the maid, Edward. Call me Abbie. Everyone else does.'

'Yes, miss.' And he blushed again.

As she went inside the house, Sarah stopped her.

'I saw yer, yer brazen hussy!'

'What are you on about, Sarah?'

'Carrying on with that 'andsome new groom!'

Abbie laughed. 'I was just saying hello, Sarah!'

'Oh yes!' Sarah raised her eyes and laughed. Then she went on, 'You're too pretty by half, Abbie 'Arris. 'E'll fall in love with you the same as every other fellow what sets eyes on you.'

'Don't talk so soft, Sarah!' said Abbie, laughing. Then she climbed the stairs up to the schoolroom to start on the day's needlework.

Mrs Plum had told her to work in the schoolroom. The light was better up there and there was much more room than in the housekeeper's little parlour downstairs.

Miss Eleanor no longer had lessons with Miss Beecham, the governess, and Miss Florrie and the younger children had no lessons in the afternoon; so if Sarah and the other under housemaid were doing other chores, Abbie was on her own. She didn't mind. She found it peaceful after all the hurly burly below stairs.

Miss Beecham had taken an interest in her, too. She sometimes gave her books to read and she had shown her different stitching and how to cut out patterns. Abbie had started making some simple clothes and Miss Beecham suggested she might start on something more complicated, so she had begun on a pretty day dress for Miss Florrie to wear at Christmas time.

Christmas.

Jim had said he'd be home by Christmas.

Abbie wanted to see Jim. Of course she did, but she was nervous, too. Nervous of how he'd be after all this time away.

But then, as the household started to prepare for Christmas, and for the homecoming of young master Percy, she was kept too busy to fret about Jim. Master Percy was eighteen now and quite the young man. Miss Florrie wanted him to escort her to balls and parties; Miss Eleanor had 'come out' last season and she was always going here and there, coming back with enticing gossip. Miss Florrie was mad with jealousy, but Miss Beecham and Lady Fanshaw both told her she must wait her turn. She would also be a debutante and be presented to the young queen, just as Eleanor had been, next season.

One afternoon, when Abbie was at her sewing, there

was a crashing up the stairs and someone hurtled into the schoolroom.

It was Master Percy.

'Where's Florrie?' he asked abruptly.

Abbie stood up and bobbed a curtsy.

'I believe she's gone visiting with Lady Fanshaw, sir,' she said.

Percy looked at her for the first time.

'That's a pretty piece of stuff you're sewing,' he said suddenly, coming towards her and feeling the material of the dress she was making between his fingers.

'Thank you, sir,' said Abbie.

'You're very neat with your fingers, aren't you, Abbie?'

'I try to please, sir.'

'Oh, come on now, Abbie, you've known me these past four years; call me Master Percy, at least.'

'Very good, Master Percy,' said Abbie, lowering her eyes.

She didn't like the way he looked at her. It made her feel uncomfortable.

He came closer and put his hand under her chin.

'My, but you're a pretty girl, Abbie.'

Abbie said nothing but she blushed deeply.

Percy laughed. 'And you've a pretty blush on your cheeks, too!' he said.

Then, still laughing, he turned and strode out of the schoolroom.

Abbie went back to her sewing, but she felt unsettled. She decided to try to avoid being alone with Master Percy in future.

But it wasn't easy. As Christmas approached, she was often alone in the schoolroom, kept busy mending and altering all the fine frocks for Miss Florrie. Because Miss Eleanor had 'come out' her dresses were made by a smart society dressmaker who came to the house for fittings. Sometimes, Abbie was asked to come and hold pins or help Miss Eleanor try on half-made frocks. She watched and learnt.

Master Percy made a habit of popping into the schoolroom when he knew he'd find her alone. Sometimes, he'd stroke her cheek or take a strand of her hair between his fingers. Sometimes he'd just smile at her and tell her what he'd been doing.

Then, one afternoon, when he came in, he was different. It was a few days before Christmas and there was such a hustle and bustle through the house. Holly festooned every nook and cranny, brought up from the country by two of the footmen who'd been sent especially to fetch it. The kitchen maids, under Mrs Flanders' eye, were busy making all kinds of sweetmeats and sugar mice and suchlike, Edward was here there and everywhere, delivering packages to other grand houses, and Mrs Flanders herself was more bad-tempered than ever, ordering quantities of poultry and meat and trying to prepare meals for the house full of family and guests.

Abbie was alone in the schoolroom, frantically trying to finish one of Miss Florrie's party frocks, when Percy burst in on her.

He'd been drinking with friends and he was unsteady and brutish, no longer satisfied with the squeeze of a hand or the stroke of a cheek.

He took the sewing from Abbie's hands and dropped it on to the floor. Then he grabbed her and forced his mouth on hers.

Abbie pushed him away, but he grabbed her again.

'Come on, my pretty,' he said. 'You know you want it!'

'No, please Master Percy,' said Abbie, gulping back the tears.

But he took no notice and started unbuttoning her blouse.

Abbie struggled and just managed to get away from him. She ran downstairs and rushed out into the mews, sobbing with fright.

As she ran on the cobbles, she slipped on some ice and fell heavily.

She hit her head as she fell and then everything went black.

When she came to, she felt sick and dizzy and, for a moment, she had no idea where she was. She looked about her, confused.

She was in the harness room, lying on a heap of hay.

Edward, the groom, was kneeling beside her, holding her hand.

'Abbie! Oh Abbie, thank the Lord you're all right.'

Abbie looked up at his kind, worried face and started to cry. Edward put his arms round her and rocked her to and fro.

Then Abbie blurted out what had happened.

'What can I do, Edward? I can't say nothing or I'll be dismissed!'

Edward put her back gently on the hay. 'We'll think of sommat,' he said, grimly. 'We'll think of sommat, Abbie.'

Just then, Jethro hobbled into the tack room.

'Abbie slipped on the ice and hit her head on the cobbles,' said Edward, hastily.

Jethro looked at her. 'Aye, I can see that,' he said. 'That's a nasty gash on yer pretty head, young Abbie.'

Abbie decided to say nothing about what had happened between her and Master Percy and she made Edward promise not to, either.

'He'd been drinking, Edward. I doubt he'll do that again.'

But she was wrong. Because she'd thwarted him, Percy wanted her more. During the next few days, he kept coming to the schoolroom, and each time she avoided him or ran away from him or made an excuse to have one of the other maids with her, it simply fuelled his passion.

Abbie confided to Edward. 'It's impossible, Edward. I feel he's watching me all the time, waiting to pounce on me.'

Edward clenched his fist. 'Young pup,' he said. 'I'd like to fight with him, man to man. Then he'd see where all his fine talk and his money gets him.'

Abbie had never heard Edward speak like that.

'You mean it, Edward, don't you?'

Edward blushed. 'I can't stand seeing you harassed like this, Abbie. I'm that fond of you.'

Abbie smiled up at him. 'I'm fond of you, too, Edward.'

In fact, she was more than fond of Edward. He was kind and steady, and he never shouted rudely after her like some of the menservants.

Suddenly, Edward started to talk. He sat her down on one of the straw bales and took her hand. He told her about his uncle, the harness-maker.

'He's brought me up, Abbie, after my mam and dad died. He never had children of his own, but he's got a good little business making harness and selling it and, one day, he says I can take over from him.'

'That would be a fine thing, Edward,' said Abbie. 'I shall just be a maid for the rest of my life.'

'No, Abbie, you won't.'

'What else could I be?'

'From what I've heard, you're a fine needlewoman.

You could be a dressmaker for the likes of Miss Eleanor and Lady Fanshaw.'

'You do talk nonsense, Edward!' said Abbie, and she stood up, loosed her hand from his and ruffled his hair.

He caught her hand again. 'You could, you know, Abbie.' Then he hesitated and blushed deeply. He stood up.

'If you'd have me, Abbie, I'd be a good husband to you.' Seeing Abbie's wide eyes, he rushed on. 'And I could be a harness-maker and you could be a dressmaker.'

Abbie looked at him. There was some straw in his hair and he had horse dung on his breeches, but to her he was the finest man in the world.

'I'd be proud to wed you, Edward,' she said.

Edward flung his arms around her and lifted her off her feet. Then he swung her round and round, nearly colliding with Jethro, who was carrying a bucket of water through the door.

'She says she'll wed me, Jethro,' shouted Edward.

A huge grin split Jethro's face. 'Well, you'll not do better than young Abbie, lad,' he said, putting down the bucket of water and slapping Edward on the back.

'Best say nothing just yet,' said Abbie, breathlessly, as Edward put her down. 'We need time to sort things.'

'Mum's the word,' said Jethro, putting his finger along the side of his nose.

Abbie was bursting with happiness, but she kept quiet. She'd need to speak to Mrs Plum and Lady Fanshaw, to get their blessing, and she'd need to take Edward to meet Mam.

Quietly, she went back into the house, tiptoeing past the open kitchen door where Mrs Flanders was yelling at all her charges. Abbie's eyes widened; she'd never seen so much food – poultry being plucked, pastry being rolled, big copper pans steaming on the hob – and she'd never seen Mrs Flanders with such a red face, either!

She went up the stairs and into the schoolroom. She took up her sewing, but her mind was so full of excitement that she did little work. She was so absorbed in her thoughts that she didn't hear Sarah coming softly up the stairs and opening the door. Her eyes were round as saucers.

'Abbie,' she whispered.

Abbie looked up. 'What is it?'

'Abbie, there's a man asking for you at the back door.'

Abbie frowned. 'A man? Who is it?'

'He looks foreign, like, with long dark 'air and wild eyes.'

Carefully, Abbie put down her sewing on the table as she tried to gather her thoughts. Foreign-looking, with wild eyes. She knew no one who could possibly fit that description, except, perhaps, one – and,

91

immediately, her instinct told her that it was him.

Sarah rushed over to her and hugged her. 'I think it's him, Abbie! I think it's your brother Jim.'

Bedford, July, present day

The first week of the holidays and we've fixed it! Katie and I have fixed to go to London on our own!

I can't believe we've done it. Katie had this brilliant idea about going back to the museum to get more stuff for our Science project.

Well, they could hardly object, could they? Keith said why couldn't we get the museum to send us stuff, but we said we needed to see all the things again. Actually, we've both finished the project and handed it in, but he doesn't know that!

Mum kept saying she'd come, too, because we didn't know London well enough.

Poor Mum. I know she's scared for me. She's terrified that we'll be mugged or raped or kidnapped. Every time I go somewhere, she doesn't relax until I'm home. But I know the other part of her wants me to learn to be independent.

So, in the end we persuaded her that, with two of us, nothing can happen and we're going with her blessing. And we've promised to keep phoning home to let her know we're OK.

I phoned to make an appointment with The London Connection and we're off tomorrow!

London, Winter 1841

'What did you say, Sarah?' whispered Abbie, clutching a piece of material between her hands.

Sarah shook her. 'I'm sure it's *JIM*! 'E says your mam sent him here!'

Slowly, Abbie got to her feet. She patted her hair and smoothed her dress.

'Come *ON*!' said Sarah impatiently, grabbing her hand and tugging her towards the door.

Abbie stumbled down the stairs and along the long stone passage to the back door.

'Go on!' said Sarah.

But as Sarah tried to push her out of the door, Abbie resisted.

'Just give me a minute, Sarah, please.'

While she stood there, preparing herself to go out into the mews and greet her brother, Abbie tried to recall his face. But, try as she might, it was indistinct. She tried to remember all they'd done together as children and, although snatches and incidents came back to her, much of it was a muddle. Would she know him, even?

Conscious of Sarah's eager eyes on her, Abbie turned the door handle and walked quietly out into the cold sunshine which struck the cobbles of the mews and glinted on the frosty patches which hadn't thawed all day.

And then she saw him, leaning against the wall, his hands in his pockets.

It was Jim all right, but oh, how he'd changed!

Gone was the skinny boy with a cheeky smiling face. Instead Abbie saw a tall, unkempt man, with greasy black hair, a straggling beard and eyes that were never still. He looked older than eighteen.

She thought her heart would burst.

'Jim!' she said quietly.

He came to her then and held both her hands, looking her up and down, not saying a word.

'Jim,' she repeated. She freed one of her hands and gently stroked his rough face.

'Abbie?' he said at last. She could hardly understand him, his voice was low and his accent that thick.

'I didn't know you at first,' he said.

Abbie nodded. 'We've both changed.'

Jim looked about him, at the beautiful house, the smart stabling, at Abbie's neat clothes.

'You've done well for yerself, Abbie,' he said. 'Quite the little lady.'

Abbie fought back the tears. 'Don't say that, Jim,' she said gently. Then she went on, 'I'm only the maid. I'm still the same.'

'But I'm not,' said Jim shortly. He pulled away from her. 'Is there any food to spare in that grand house of yours?'

If Abbie was hurt by his rough response to her after all this time, she didn't let on.

'I'll see what I can find,' she said. She hesitated. 'Do you want to come in the kitchen?'

He shook his head. 'I'd not fit in,' he muttered.

Abbie didn't argue. 'Stay here, then, I won't be long.'

Nervously, Abbie went into the kitchen, hoping that Mrs Flanders might be consulting with the housekeeper or Lady Fanshaw, as she did frequently now that Christmas was almost here. Abbie hoped that she could persuade one of the kitchen maids to let her have something for Jim. But Mrs Flanders was there, as large as life. And Christmas time was not a good time to ask Mrs Flanders a favour.

'Mrs Flanders,' she began, nervously.

'Yes, what is it? Can't you see I'm busy, girl?'

'My brother's at the back door,' she began.

'Your brother. First I'd heard of a brother!'

'He's a sailor,' said Abbie, blushing furiously. 'He's come to see me and . . .'

'And I suppose he's hungry?'

Abbie nodded.

Mrs Flanders huffed and puffed, but eventually she produced some bread and some cheese and handed it over. Then she followed Abbie down the passage.

'This is not to happen again,' she warned. 'I'm not going to make a habit of feeding rough sailors from

95

my kitchen, especially not at Christmas time, when I'm dead on my feet.'

'No, Mrs Flanders,' said Abbie, meekly.

Abbie jumped. Jim had come inside and was lurking in the passage, half hidden in the shadows. If Abbie hadn't known him, she would have been scared by his brooding presence.

Mrs Flanders stopped dead and looked at him long and hard, then she turned on her heel and went back to the kitchen.

Jim took the food and began stuffing it into his mouth.

'Jim,' said Abbie, nervously, 'you can't stay here or I'll get in trouble.'

'Trouble, eh?' said Jim, between mouthfuls. 'Don't tell me about trouble.'

Abbie hung her head. 'I'm sorry, Jim. I didn't mean . . . I want to know,' said Abbie. 'I want to know all about it. We've got so much catching up to do. You'll have so much to tell me.'

Jim went on eating.

'Look, I'm off next Thursday noon, after Christmas. Can you come here and we'll walk back to Mam's together?'

Jim shrugged. 'Yeah,' he said. 'Yeah, I'll come if I can.' He hesitated and looked straight at her for the first time. 'But I've got some scores to settle first. I'll come if I can. If you want.'

Jim finished the bread and wiped his mouth on his sleeve. Abbie glanced behind her, towards the kitchen.

'You'd better go, Jim.'

He sniffed. 'Don't worry, Abbie, I'll not trouble you any longer. You and your fine friends.'

Abbie sighed. 'It's not . . .'

But he cut her short, took her hand and squeezed it and turned for the back door. She followed him and they spoke for a couple of minutes out in the mews.

Just before he left, Jim said, 'Who's that pretty little wench that opened the door to me? And wot's been staring at me from the winder?'

Abbie looked up just in time to see Sarah's face disappearing hastily from the landing window upstairs. She smiled. 'That's Sarah,' she said. 'She's my friend.'

Jim grunted. And then he was gone.

Abbie didn't go inside immediately. She ran to the stables to find Edward. But he was out with the carriage. She'd told him about Jim. She had no secrets from Edward and she wanted to tell him what had happened.

And, of course, she'd told Sarah, too. She hoped Sarah would have the sense to keep her mouth shut about where Jim had been these last six years.

When she walked past the kitchen to go upstairs to the schoolroom again, Mrs Flanders was standing in the doorway, her arms folded.

'Thank you for the food, Mrs Flanders,' said Abbie. Mrs Flanders said nothing.

Bedford, July, present day

It's past midnight but I can't sleep. I've just got to write this down or I'll burst.

I haven't found him or anything, but I think we may be on to something. It's only a little tiny glimmer, but maybe . . . It's better than anything else, anyway.

Me and Katie had quite a scary time in London. We'd never been to London on our own and we didn't really have a clue, even though we pretended we knew where we were going and how to get there. Poor Mum drew all these maps and went over and over the underground route, but, of course, we weren't going where she thought we were, so it was a waste of time. But we couldn't exactly tell her that, could we?

Mum had had Matt's photo sent all over and I was going to nick a copy of that to take to London with me. But when I came to look at it, I didn't think it was like how I remembered him.

Just before he left I'd taken some shots of Matt and the rest of the band, when they were rehearsing. Matt had asked me to take them with his camera; I think he was hoping to use them for publicity or something.

Anyway, there was one of Matt playing the keyboard and singing. It just looked so like him — just as I'd remembered him — that I decided it would be that photo I'd take with me.

It was good I had Katie. I would have panicked otherwise. We got lost on the tube — went the wrong way, twice — then we thought some mad old guy was following us.

Anyway, when we reached Charing Cross, we found this place – The London Connection – quite easily.

All around there, and near the big church beside it, there were groups of homeless people. Well, I suppose they were homeless. Most of them were men and they were sitting or lying on the steps of the church. Many of them were drinking. Some had dogs with them, some were sleeping, wrapped up in a coat or blanket.

I noticed someone come up with a hose and start sluicing the street. There was a nasty stink of wee.

I was scared and I was really glad that Katie was with me. All the way up on the train, we'd been giggling and telling each other jokes. But there wasn't much to laugh about here and we fell silent.

The London Connection was just round the corner from the church, in Adelaide Street. We walked up the steps to a big blue door.

It was bolted, but there was an intercom, so I took a deep breath and spoke into it. There was a bit of a wait, but then we were let in.

It was dingy inside, but the young man at the reception was friendly enough. He said someone would come and see us in a minute.

While we were waiting, we could see some of these people in the next room. It seemed to be a sort of games room; there was a pool table and table tennis. There were lots of young men and women in there, but they didn't take much notice of us.

I hung around at the door and peered in, feeling embarrassed. I looked quickly at the people in there, but Matt wasn't one of them. I hadn't really expected to find him here, but I couldn't help a pang of disappointment.

Then a man came down the stairs and into reception. He was quite young and very friendly. He told us that he worked for The London Connection and he'd be happy to have a chat.

We followed him up three flights of stairs. It was a huge, grim old building and there was a cabbagey smell about it, but there was a buzz about it, too.

We got to a sort of landing place and sat down at a table. The man brought us plastic cups of tea from a machine. People were coming and going all the time and he often said 'hi' to them as they passed.

He asked how he could help, so I started. I showed him the photo of Matt and explained what had happened.

He stared at the photo for some time and then he handed it back, but his face gave nothing away.

'Has he been here?' I blurted out.

The man looked at me and smiled.

'Becky,' he said. 'Young people are here because they know they are safe and they know that we will never betray their confidence.'

My face must have shown my disappointment.

'So, even if you knew he'd been here, you wouldn't say?'

He shook his head. 'Never.' He took a sip of tea. 'We take people here from sixteen to twenty-five, from all sorts of backgrounds, for all sorts of reasons. Unless they ask us to contact their friends and families, we respect their privacy. We have to, Becky, otherwise they would never trust us.'

'What happens if they've been in trouble with the police?' I knew my voice was shaking, but I had to know the answer.

The man smiled again. 'A lot of the young people who come here have been in trouble with the police, Becky. We have a special unit to liaise with the police, and we can find out exactly what the charges are against a young person and what is likely to happen to them. And often, it isn't half as bad as they think.'

'So do you make them go to the police, then?'

The man nodded. 'If they want to keep coming here, then they must co-operate with the police. But they are given a lot of help from a lot of very understanding people.'

'So if Matt had been here,' I said slowly, 'he'd have found out that they'd caught the bloke who took the stuff from the school?'

'If he'd been here,' said the man, 'he'd know exactly what had happened.'

He was looking me straight in the eye when he said this. I was sure, then, that he knew where Matt was. It was such a relief to think that Matt almost certainly knew that the police didn't want him, that I started to cry.

Katie handed me a wodge of tissues. She could see that I couldn't speak, so she jumped in.

'What happens when someone like Matt runs away?' she asked. 'I mean, if he comes to London?'

'Well, every night and every morning, our workers go to all the mainline railway stations and, if they see a young person who looks vulnerable, they will approach them and try to persuade them to come to a hostel for the time being, where they'll be safe.'

'So they don't sleep here, then?'

'No, we are just a centre where young people come during the day. As soon as we find them, or they make contact with us, we get them into hostels where they can sleep and be fed.'

'But what do they do for money?' said Katie.

'We help them get ID and apply for their allowances from the State.'

'Without going to their families?'

'Without going to their families, unless they want us to.'

'And what then?' asked Katie. 'Do they stay in hostels for ever?'

'No. They often get into other housing, with other youngsters. But there is always someone to help them, someone who goes to see them regularly, until they are back on their feet.'

By this time, I'd stopped crying. I rubbed my eyes.

'What about a job?' I asked. 'Would you help with that?'

'With a sixteen-year-old, we'd try and help them get back to school. We can't always persuade them to do this, but, if they have no qualifications, then it's hard to find work for them.'

'So, would it be a school in London?'

'Yes, a school near the hostel.'

'Where are the hostels?' I'd blurted it out. I couldn't help myself.

The man smiled. 'We use hostels all over the city, Becky.'

He wasn't going to give any more away.

He got up then. 'Would you like to have a look round?' he said.

We nodded and got up and then he took us for a quick tour. It was a warren of a place, up and down stairs, in and out of big communal rooms. We saw an art room and a music room. In the art room there were some quite scary pictures and I couldn't help wondering about the people who had done them. What had they been through? There were a lot of pictures about prison, too.

The music room was locked but, even so, I peered hopefully in through a window.

We went back to the reception desk. The man said goodbye and we thanked him. It was funny. I don't think I've ever felt such trust for anyone. If he knew Matt, if Matt has been helped by someone like him, then perhaps he'll be OK.

As we were turning for the front door, I put my hand into my bag and took out a letter.

'I know you can't say anything,' I said. 'I understand that. But, just in case you see Matt . . .' I hesitated. Then I handed him the photo and the letter.

He didn't say anything. But he took them.

* * *

We came out into the street, blinking in the sunshine and smelling the acrid smell of unwashed bodies as we walked back past the church again to the tube.

We didn't say much at first. We were both a bit stunned. Then Katie looked at her watch.

'Hey, we'd better hurry,' she said.

We legged it for the Science Museum to pick up some leaflets, just so we could pretend we'd spent the day there. At the tube station, I thought we might see the boy, huddled in his corner, but there was no sign of him.

Needless to say, we got lost again, but, in the end, we made it back home on the right train.

I don't know why I feel so good about this. It's not a breakthrough or anything. Far from it. And God knows whether the man at the London Connection does know anything about Matt or whether he'll pass on my letter.

Probably by tomorrow I'll be really down about it again.

It's daft, I know, but right now, for the first time since Matt left, I feel there's some hope that we'll find him. I'm really glad we went to that place.

5

London, Winter 1841

Christmas Day arrived at last. In the morning, the whole household was summoned to the front hall.

Most of the servants never went near the front hall; their life was lived behind the green baize door leading to the servants' quarters and the back stairs.

Abbie and Sarah lined up neatly with all the others, and Lord and Lady Fanshaw, Master Percy, Miss Eleanor, Miss Florrie and all the smaller Fanshaw children came down the front stairs to greet them. Abbie had often seen Lady Fanshaw, of course, but she'd hardly ever set eyes on Lord Fanshaw. She curtsyed shyly, like all the other women, and then stood quietly, her hands folded in front of her.

Each one of the servants was handed a small gift. Lady Fanshaw gave Abbie hers. Abbie took it and blushed.

'Thank you, ma'am,' she said.

Lady Fanshaw smiled. 'You deserve it, Abbie.'

Later, in a few moments of privacy, Abbie undid the package. Inside was a beautifully worked needlecase, with a whole set of needles in it. Abbie gasped. She'd never owned such a beautiful thing. She thought sadly of Mam, spending Christmas with neighbours. Abbie had made her a sampler to hang over her bed. She knew Mam would be pleased with it. She wondered, briefly, where Jim was spending Christmas. When she'd asked him, he had just told her that he had his own plans.

The rest of the day was a blur of activity. At noon, the servants had their own Christmas dinner, presided over by Mrs Plum and the butler, and then, in the evening, the family and their visitors had a feast which made Abbie's eyes goggle.

Soups first, then fish, then vegetables and sauces and the poultry, all went up from the kitchen, carried on silver dishes by the footmen, then the used china and glasses and silver came down again before the great Christmas pudding went up and the blancmange and jellies, followed by nuts and sweetmeats.

All the servants were put to work to help and there was little room in the kitchen to turn round. Abbie and Sarah washed dishes for most of the evening, but they both felt the excitement of the occasion and, when they finally retired to their attic room to sleep, they were full of gossip and giggles.

At last, just as Abbie was dropping off to sleep, Sarah said, 'It was a happy day, Abbie.'

'It was that,' said Abbie, yawning.

She wondered if Jim's day had been so full and happy.

Jim didn't turn up the next Thursday, but Edward was free so Abbie took him to meet Mam. She seemed to like him and be pleased that Abbie would settle down.

Mrs Plum was really nice, too, when Abbie, falteringly, told her about Edward's proposal. She even gave Abbie a hug; Abbie was so surprised she stood for a moment, unable to say a thing.

'I'm that pleased for you both, Abbie,' said Mrs Plum, still holding Abbie's shoulders. 'He's a steady young lad and he'll make something of himself, you mark my words.'

'One day, he'll take over his uncle's harness-making business,' said Abbie proudly, when she'd recovered herself.

'And I hope you'll keep on with your needlework, Abbie. I hear such good things from the young ladies and Lady Fanshaw.'

'Yes, Mrs Plum, I hope to.' Abbie bit her lip. 'Mrs Plum?'

'Yes, my dear?'

'Do you think, one day – not yet, of course, but one day – I could set up as a dressmaker?'

Mrs Plum looked at her shrewdly.

'Well, I'd never have thought about it myself, dear, but I don't see why not.'

'It . . . well, it was Edward's idea,' said Abbie, blushing.

'And not a bad idea at that,' said Mrs Plum. Then she went on, 'Would you like me to speak to Lady Fanshaw about it? She's seen your work and perhaps she could recommend you to her friends.'

'Oh Mrs Plum, I'd be ever so grateful . . .'

'I can't promise anything, Abbie, but, if I find the right time, I'll mention it.'

She was as good as her word and it was not long before Lady Fanshaw sent for Abbie.

'Let me tell you what I've done, Abbie,' said Lady Fanshaw.

Abbie bobbed a curtsy.

'I've spoken to my own dressmaker and she's happy to teach you all she knows. She's not as young as she was and her eyes are getting weak. She says she'd welcome some help from a neat sewer. Then, perhaps, one day, you can take on some of her customers.'

'Thank you, Lady Fanshaw. Thank you very much.'

As soon as she had a free moment, Abbie rushed out into the mews to tell Edward, but she was just out the back door when someone called to her.

'Abbie!' She heard a voice but saw no one.

Then Jim emerged from the shadows.

'Jim, how you startled me!'

Jim walked over to her.

'I came to say I'll walk back home with you to Mam's next Thursday noon if you're free.'

'Oh Jim! That's good.'

'And I've got sommat to show you.'

He fished into the pocket of his grimy smock and drew something out.

'Shut yer eyes and 'old out yer 'ands.'

Obediently, Abbie did as she was told, but she felt frightened. There was something threatening about Jim. Whatever he had to show her, it wouldn't be a simple present, she knew that.

'Now yer can look.'

She looked and her eyes widened. 'Oh Jim, it's not?'

He grinned. 'I've sweated six years for the damn thing. Thought I might as well 'ave it.'

In her hands was a gold watch attached to a heavy gold chain. With trembling fingers, Abbie turned it over and read the inscription on the back: 'To my son, Charles Frobisher, on the occasion of his marriage. From his father. June 1830.'

'But how . . . ?'

'Told you I had scores to settle, didn't I? Well, I ran that Greasy Will to earth.'

'Greasy Will! But he disappeared. The costers were after him.'

'I got contacts, Abbie. Not the sort of folk you'd

know.' He laughed, but there was no humour in it. 'I found the little weasel.'

'Jim, what did you do to him?' whispered Abbie.

Jim shrugged. ' 'E was already nearly dead – and deranged. I shook 'im up a bit and 'e begged me to take the watch. Said it was the beginning of his bad luck.'

Jim took the watch from Abbie's hands. 'Bad luck!' He spat on the cobbles with contempt. 'What does 'e know of bad luck!'

'Jim,' said Abbie gently.

For the first time, Jim's eyes met hers.

'I know, Abbie. It's not your fault I've become what I am. But I'm trouble; I'll only make you fret, you and Mam. It's best you forget me.'

'Jim! You've only just come home. Please don't talk like that.'

Jim sniffed and said nothing.

'We had some good times together, Jim, working on the market and that,' Abbie pleaded.

Jim nodded. 'I went up Whitechapel Market,' he said suddenly. 'But I didn't know the people any more.'

'Lil died not long after you . . . after you left.'

Jim nodded. 'Everything changes, Abbie. We can't stand still. The past was then. Now is now. Everything's changed.'

Abbie didn't know what to say. Part of her desperately wanted the old Jim back, but she knew it would never be – and she had to admit that she was scared of this harsh, rough fellow standing beside her.

'I've got to go now,' said Jim, breaking the silence. I'll see you Thursday.'

He turned from her and then, without a further word, he walked off.

Suddenly Abbie's good news about dressmaking lessons didn't seem very important. With a heavy heart, she watched him round the corner out of the mews, then she went back inside the house.

Sarah met her outside the kitchen door.

'That was Jim, wasn't it?' she said. 'Oo, 'e's that 'andsome!'

Mrs Flanders was sitting at the kitchen table. The door was open and she overheard.

'That the sailor brother of yours, Abbie, lurking round here again?'

' 'E's come all the way from Australia,' said Sarah. 'Been away six years.'

Mrs Flanders got up slowly from the table.

'Six years,' she said slowly. 'Is that so?'

Abbie felt as though someone had punched her in the stomach.

Mrs Flanders knew. She knew that Jim was no sailor. Who else would she tell? Would she spread the story round the household? The story that nice, reliable, steady young Abbie had a criminal for a brother?

Thursday was bright and cold. There were still visitors at the house in Cavendish Square and the maids were kept very busy. Abbie felt quite guilty slipping away at noon for her half-day.

This time Jim was as good as his word. He was there, out in the mews. Abbie glanced anxiously across at the stables. Although Edward knew all about Jim, she'd not introduced them. And she'd not told Jim about Edward and their plans to get wed, though she supposed Mam might have said something.

She'd tell him all about Edward today.

At first they walked in silence. Once or twice, Abbie tried to start a conversation, but Jim had only grunted in reply.

'What's the matter?' Abbie said at last.

'I want to get back to where I feel comfortable,' said Jim shortly. 'I can't abide these grand streets and big houses.'

They'd nearly reached Mam's lodgings when Jim suddenly stopped.

'Let's stay 'ere by the river for a bit,' he said.

Neither suggested it, but, instinctively they turned and walked down to the Tower Steps.

'The old river's full of memories, eh?' said Jim.

Abbie nodded. 'Not such good ones for you.'

Jim shrugged. 'I dunno. We had some good times, you and me and Mam and Pa.'

Abbie smiled. 'We did.'

Jim stared over the water.

Abbie touched his arm. 'Tell me about it, Jim. Tell me about Van Diemen's Land.'

He turned and looked at her then and she found it hard to read the expression in his eyes.

'You couldn't begin to imagine it, Abbie.'

'I'll try,' she said simply. 'Please.'

'All right. If you're sure you want to hear.'

And then, slowly at first, Jim started to speak. Once he'd started, the words tumbled out and Abbie could sense the rage inside him.

'I was that scared, Abbie, when they put me in Millbank. To be sure I was cheeky and a smart lad, but I wasn't really bad like some of those in with me. And all the time, I knew I'd done nothing wrong. All the time I thought I'd be freed.'

'We tried,' said Abbie. 'But it seemed we couldn't do nothing for you.'

'Nah! There's no justice for the likes of us. If you're poor and you gets in trouble, then no one cares.'

'The costers tried.'

'Yeah, they tried. But they were up against those damn bobbies and no one believed the costers. Everyone believed Frobisher and his toffy friends.'

Abbie nodded and they were both silent for a while.

'What was it like – the voyage?' asked Abbie at last.

'It was hell,' said Jim, simply. 'It took months. We

were sick as dogs, all kept below decks in stinking filth, chained up like animals.'

Abbie shuddered. 'Did you never see daylight?'

'Once a day,' said Jim, smiling grimly. 'Once a day, we shuffled round the deck, with guards prodding and poking at us.'

'Did you get sick?'

'Everyone was sick, Abbie. Some were sick because of the roll of the sea, lots of the men were sick before they left. They got worse and died of disease on the voyage, tossed into the sea like so many dead rats.'

'Was there no one who treated you well?'

Jim scratched his beard. 'There was one guard on the ship. He was the only one that treated me like a human being. The guards weren't supposed to talk to us, but he sometimes gave me a smile and a few words of encouragement if no one was looking. I think he felt sorry for me; I was so small beside some of the great hulking men.'

Jim picked up a stone and tossed it into the river. They watched, in silence, as the ripples spread out from it and then subsided.

'Yeah, he was the only guard with an ounce of kindness in him. Sometimes he'd tell me about the island where we were going. He made it sound warm and friendly, like. Sometimes, the thought of that warm and friendly island was all that kept me going.'

'And when you reached Van Dieman's Land, was it like that?'

'Huh! It was warm all right – but only in the summer. We fried in the summer and froze in the winter, with the winds whipping up from the ocean. We just had a bit of sacking for a sort of hammock to sleep in and we could never keep warm in the winter. And it certainly wasn't friendly. That hell-hole Point Puer was the bleakest place on earth. There was no fresh water there and the ground was too stony to grow much, so all the supplies came by boat from Port Arthur.'

'Point Puer,' repeated Abbie. She'd often thought about it, in that faraway country of Van Diemen's Land on the other side of the world. She'd even found Van Diemen's Land, marked in pink on the globe of the world that stood on the teacher's table at the church school. But knowing where it was didn't help her much. She still couldn't begin to imagine how it would look or what birds or animals lived there.

Jim squatted down, his back to a lamppost, and ran some dirt through his hand.

'Point Puer was a prison for lads, Abbie. Boys from twelve to eighteen. It jutted out on a piece of land into the sea, just across the water from Port Arthur, the men's prison.'

Abbie didn't say anything. She'd never seen the sea. She'd never been away from London.

Jim went on. 'Some of the lads were already young villains and they were rough and cruel themselves. Point Puer was supposed to reform them by teaching them a trade and how to read and write.'

'That was good, wasn't it?' said Abbie.

Jim snorted. 'There was only an hour of school, mostly in the evenings, and the trades were taught by convicts from Port Arthur. But there weren't enough convicts who had a trade to teach.'

'Did *you* learn a trade?'

Jim nodded. 'To begin with. I was learning to be a carpenter, but then one of the other boys got me into trouble and my training stopped. Learning a trade was a privilege and if there was any sign of trouble the privilege was stopped.'

'Did you make anything?'

'Yeah. I helped put up some of the buildings. We had to do everything for ourselves. The boys learning to be tailors had to make clothes for us, cobblers the boots and so on. And those learning to be stonemasons shaped the stones for the church over at Port Arthur.'

'So what did you do if you weren't learning a trade?'

'Cleaned out the place, broke stones, levelled the ground. Back-breaking, relentless work. Day after day, week after week. They could always find us work, Abbie.'

'Didn't you have any free time?'

'Yeah. We had time to ourselves, too, but that was

when the rough lads did most of their bullying. They'd seek you out and set on you, if you'd done sommat they didn't like.'

They were both silent for a while, Jim reliving his time at Point Puer and Abbie trying to imagine how it had been for him, how it had changed him.

Jim broke the silence. 'And just over the water, where we could see it, was the huge men's prison at Port Arthur. A great threat hanging over us. That's what it was.'

He shivered suddenly, then went on. 'Poor wretches. Sometimes, if the wind were in the right direction, we'd hear the screams of the men being flogged. They did the floggings before church on Sunday mornings.'

He tossed his handful of dirt into the river. 'None of us wanted to go on to Port Arthur,' he said. 'However bad it was at Point Puer, it couldn't be as bad as the prison over the water.'

'Did they beat *you?*' asked Abbie.

Jim shrugged. 'It were only supposed to be after they'd tried other punishments – solitary confinement, diet of bread and water, extra duties, that sort of thing. But yeah, we got beat all right. But not like the men. Not strung up on a triangle and flogged until the skin came off yer back.'

Abbie felt sick.

'Most of the overseers at Point Puer came from Port Arthur. They were convicts themselves and none too gentle. They'd lay into us with a stick sometimes.'

'What for?'

'What for? They didn't need no excuse, Abbie. For not learning yer lessons right, for not working quick enough when you were chopping wood or breaking stones. Some of them were vicious and enjoyed seeing us cowed and whipped.'

'Were there no kind men?'

Jim looked away into the distance. 'Yeah, some were good to us. They weren't all like that. The surgeon weren't a bad fellow. He'd patch you up if one of the overseers had been too free with the birch and he'd sometimes have the fellow up on a charge. But if that happened, the overseer would bide his time and get back at you worse than ever. Yer learnt to keep your mouth shut over there Abbie, I can tell you.'

'Did you make any friends there? Any of the other lads?'

'Huh. It didn't do to get close to others. It were soon spotted and they split you up.'

Jim stood up again and stretched. 'Though there was one lad – poor dolt.'

'Who was that?'

'He was a country lad and a bit soft. He couldn't do his lessons and he just got more and more confused and frightened. The convict schoolmaster who taught us 'ad a terrible temper. He'd shout at the poor boy and whip him for not learning his letters, so, in the end, I tried to teach him a bit – secretly like.'

'Did it help him?'

'Aye, a bit, but the master still went after him. And in the end, he couldn't take any more.'

'What happened?'

'He ran away.'

'Did he escape?'

'Nah, course he didn't. There was no fresh water nearby and there was thick undergrowth and sharp rocks everywhere. And even if he 'ad got clear, all the ways off the peninsular were guarded.

'So . . .'

Jim sighed. 'After two days, they found him. He was senseless and parched and out of his wits with terror. So they revived him enough to give him a public beating, in front of all of us.'

Abbie clutched Jim's arm. 'That's horrible!'

Jim nodded. 'It was a horrible place, Abbie.'

'And what happened to the boy?'

'He died,' said Jim, shortly, and he turned his face away from Abbie and looked out over the river. Abbie didn't dare to ask how he had died.

She was close to tears. Poor Jim. He'd seen sights no boy should have witnessed. He'd started out a loving lad, full of cheek and swagger, and returned this bitter young man with a head full of vile memories.

'But it's over now Jim.'

Jim rounded on her. 'Oh yes, Abbie, it's over. I

behaved myself and did as I was bid. I kept me mouth shut and worked hard so I'd get my ticket of leave home, but there wasn't one day when I didn't plan my revenge on the folk who put me through it.'

'Greasy Will?'

'Him! He's just a raving bag of bones, now. But there's others.'

'Jim. Forget them! It's all behind you. You can earn a decent wage now. Get on and live a free life again.' She hesitated. 'I'll help you – and Mam – and, and Edward.'

'Oh yes, your fine upstanding young man. Mam's told me all about him.' Jim blew his nose into his hand and smeared the snot down the side of his breeches.

Abbie ignored this.

'We'll help you, Jim.'

Jim rounded on her, suddenly. His eyes flashed with anger and Abbie drew back, frightened. This was the other Jim. The Jim that frightened her.

'Don't you understand, you stupid chit! I'm marked! I'll never be able to make an honest wage. I'm a criminal and I'll be treated as a criminal for the rest of my life.'

Abbie said nothing.

'Let's go and see Mam,' said Jim, gruffly.

They spent an hour or so with Mam but Abbie could see she was worried about Jim, too.

'Why don't you lodge here with me, Jim?' she asked.

'No, Mam, I've got a place to go.'

'Where, Jim?'

'What yer don't know can't harm yer.' And that was all he would say.

Abbie had to get back to Cavendish Square before dark. The winter day was short, so she left Mam's place earlier than she would have wished.

'I'll come with you, Abbie,' said Jim.

Mam looked relieved. 'Yes, you do that,' she said. But Abbie wasn't sure if Mam was pleased that she had company on the long walk back or pleased not to be alone with Jim.

'She's getting old,' said Jim, as they walked along the riverside.

'Mam?'

Jim nodded. 'She was always so full of life and now . . . I dunno, Abbie. She's bent and she doesn't see so well.'

Abbie was shocked.

'Mam? But she's not old!'

She hadn't noticed any change in Mam, but then she'd seen her every two weeks, without fail. And sometimes, if Mam had to deliver some mending up West, she'd call at the house in Cavendish Square. Mrs Plum liked Mam and she'd sometimes even invite her into her parlour for a chat.

Jim's words echoed round her head. 'Doesn't see so

121

well.' Just what Lady Fanshaw had said about her smart dressmaker.

How long would Mam be able to go on with her mending?

Jim didn't speak much on the way back, but he came right to the door.

'Thanks, Jim.' Abbie hesitated. 'Will you come with me again next time?'

But Jim wasn't listening. He was looking up at the window above the back door from which an eager young face was peering down.

'Oi, Sarah,' he shouted. 'Come down 'ere!'

The face disappeared and, seconds later, a breathless Sarah arrived at the back door. Rather reluctantly, Abbie introduced her to Jim.

Jim looked her up and down. It reminded her of the way that Master Percy had looked and it made her uneasy.

'Off yer go then, Abbie,' said Jim. 'I've got some private business with young Sarah.'

Abbie frowned. 'Sarah,' she said sharply, 'you should be at your work.'

'You should be at your work,' mimicked Jim, still looking at Sarah. 'Leave 'er be, Abbie. You're too bossy by half.'

Abbie blushed, but she said nothing and went quietly inside.

London, 1842

The Christmas period had passed, with its flurry of activity, with parties and balls and comings and goings. Master Percy was back from his regiment and the house was often full of his friends. There was a rumour he had taken up with some society woman as a mistress. Whether this was true or not, he'd lost interest in Abbie, much to her relief.

For most of the time, Abbie was too busy to worry about Jim. Once or twice, he'd arrive at the back door on her afternoon off and they'd go to see Mam. But, as the year wore on, it happened less and less.

But he was walking out with Sarah and Abbie was worried. She didn't want to spoil Sarah's fun but she watched, uneasily, as Sarah left the house on her afternoon off. She felt like a spy, seeing them slink away together, down the mews, Jim's arm around Sarah's slim waist, stopping to kiss when they thought they were out of sight.

Then Sarah would come back in the evening, flushed and bright-eyed.

Abbie spoke to her mam about it one day.

'He's that bitter, Mam,' she said. 'He's all twisted up inside. And she just sees his 'andsome face and flashing eyes.'

'Maybe she'll calm him down, then,' said Mam.

Abbie shook her head. 'You don't know her,

Mam. She's that headstrong herself.'

And she tried to talk to Sarah about Jim.

'You be careful, Sarah, please,' said Abbie.

'What's the matter, Abbie, don't you trust your own brother!'

'He's wild, Sarah. He'll break your heart.'

'I like 'em wild,' retorted Sarah. 'Anyway, 'e's a sight more fun than that boring Edward of yours.'

Abbie sighed. Sarah had changed since she'd taken up with Jim; she challenged Abbie when she asked her to do things, she became sloppy in her work, and she was more dreamy than ever. But there was no reasoning with her.

Jim was making things difficult for Abbie. And not just with Sarah.

One day, when she was passing the kitchen, she heard Mrs Flanders talking to some of the other servants.

'Huh! He's no sailor. He's a returned convict. He's no good, that young man, and I don't like him hanging round the house.'

Gradually, the atmosphere changed. The other servants were less open with Abbie. But Mrs Plum was her constant ally. One day, she came up to the schoolroom to talk to Abbie.

'Is it true, Abbie, what they're saying about your brother?'

Abbie hung her head. 'Yes,' she whispered.

Mrs Plum sat down heavily at the table. 'He's not a sailor, then?'

Abbie shook her head. 'I'm sorry I lied to you, Mrs Plum.'

Mrs Plum smiled. 'If you'd told me he'd been transported, I'd not have taken you on, Abbie, and that would have been our loss.'

Abbie looked up. 'He was wrongly accused, Mrs Plum. And . . . and he's had a terrible time.'

Mrs Plum patted her hand. 'None of it is your fault, Abbie. Nor your mam's.'

'The others talk about him behind my back,' said Abbie sadly.

Mrs Plum got up. 'Then they should know better,' she said firmly.

But once the story was out, Abbie could feel the suspicion around her.

If anything went missing, there was always the unspoken thought that Jim might have taken it – or Abbie, even. She knew that some of the older servants blamed her for introducing Sarah to Jim – for letting him come to the house in the first place. Once she came upon a couple of the younger maids whispering together in a corner and then, when they saw her, they immediately stopped talking and stared at the ground. But she could feel their eyes follow her as she passed and she knew they'd been gossiping about Jim.

She'd always been so happy at Cavendish Square,

but now every day she worried; worried about Jim and Sarah, worried about what people were saying and worried about her mam, too, who was suddenly becoming very frail.

Edward was her rock. He refused to listen to gossip about Jim and Sarah and he always stood up for Abbie. Without Edward, her life would have been impossible.

And without the support of Lady Fanshaw and Mrs Plum.

Miss Florrie was to 'come out' this season and Lady Fanshaw had entrusted all the dressmaking to Abbie.

This was her first really big challenge. She tried not to think of all the grand places her dresses and capes would be seen and simply got on with the work, cutting and pinning, fitting and sewing.

In the days before the first ball of the season, Miss Florrie was in such a state that Abbie had trouble getting her to stand still.

'Please, Miss Florrie, stop all this wriggling,' she begged, kneeling down to check how the material fell. 'You mother's coming in a moment to see the ball gown.'

'Oh Abbie, will anyone want to dance with me? Am I pretty enough?'

Abbie smiled up at the girl. Florrie had a flawless complexion and glossy dark hair which fell about her shoulders in ringlets. Abbie turned her towards the mirror.

'Look in there, Miss Florrie,' said Abbie, 'and tell me what you see.'

Florrie pouted.

'I suppose I'll do,' she said, grinning.

'You'll have every young man in London swooning at your feet, Miss Florrie,' said Abbie. 'You mark my words.'

Florrie giggled, and Abbie straightened the final flounce on the gown just as Lady Fanshaw came into the room.

Lady Fanshaw stopped dead and her hand flew to her mouth.

'Oh Florrie, dear, you look quite beautiful!'

Lady Fanshaw was not given to extravagant compliments and both Florrie and Abbie were surprised.

Abbie recovered first. She got up off her knees and bobbed a quick curtsy. 'Doesn't she just, ma'am. She'll do you proud.'

Lady Fanshaw smiled and Abbie was sure that there was a tear in her eye.

'And she'll do *you* proud, too, Abbie. That is a beautiful gown.'

'Thank you, ma'am,' said Abbie, simply.

A few days later, Abbie dressed Florrie and escorted her downstairs to the carriage which was waiting outside the front door. She helped her into the seat, making sure that the gown wasn't crushed. Florrie, with her cape round her shoulders, her mother's jewels in her hair and with spotless white gloves on her hands, looked stunning.

Lord and Lady Fanshaw got in after her and even Lord Fanshaw was taken aback.

'My, my, little Florrie. Quite the lady now,' he said gruffly.

Edward closed the carriage door, winked at Abbie and mounted the box in front, then, with a soft 'Gerrrup' to the horses, they were off, clattering through the square.

Abbie had promised to stay up late to wait for Miss Florrie's return that night. She and Mrs Plum sat in Mrs Plum's room and chatted the evening away.

At last they heard the carriage return.

'Will we go to the front door?' said Mrs Plum.

Abbie shook her head. 'No, perhaps it's best to wait here.' She hesitated. 'Just in case the evening wasn't . . .'

But she need not have worried. There was a shout from the main hall.

'Abbie! Abbie, where are you?'

Abbie and Mrs Plum went quickly into the hall and Florrie, with eyes shining, came running towards them. She hugged Abbie.

'Abbie, it was a triumph, to be sure. I promise you, I was the belle of the ball. Everyone said it. And they all admired my dress and asked for the name of my dressmaker.'

'Oh, Miss Florrie, I'm that pleased for you,' said Abbie, taking the girl's hands in hers. Then, laughing, Miss Florrie twirled her round and round until they were both quite giddy and out of breath.

A few days later, Lady Fanshaw sent for Abbie.

'Florrie's gowns have been much admired, Abbie,' she said.

'Oh, I'm so pleased, ma'am,' said Abbie.

'In fact,' said Lady Fanshaw, 'at her coming out ball, several ladies of my acquaintance asked me for the name of her dressmaker.'

Abbie smiled.

Lady Fanshaw looked at her keenly. 'Mrs Plum has been speaking to me. Perhaps the time has come, Abbie, for you to set yourself up as a dressmaker.' Then she went on, before Abbie could reply: 'When are you and Edward planning to get married?'

Abbie blushed. 'When you give us leave, ma'am. We'd not want to do anything without your permission.'

'And where will you live?'

'Above his uncle's shop, ma'am. His uncle is a harness-maker in East Smithfield.'

'East Smithfield,' repeated Lady Fanshaw.

Abbie smiled secretly to herself. She doubted Lady Fanshaw had even the vaguest idea where East Smithfield was.

'Not far from the Tower, ma'am, near to my mam's lodgings,' she said, helpfully.

'Quite so,' said Lady Fanshaw. 'And Edward has agreed this with Jethro and with Lord Fanshaw?'

'I believe so, ma'am. Edward's uncle wants him to learn the trade and be apprenticed to him. And Lord Fanshaw says he can give him some work mending leather and suchlike.' Abbie looked down at her hands. 'Of course, he'll wait until another groom's in place, ma'am, and until Lord Fanshaw says he may go.'

'And you'll go with our blessing,' said Lady Fanshaw. 'I shall speak with my husband, but I should say that August would be a good time, at the end of the Season, when we leave for the country.'

'Thank you, ma'am.'

Abbie waited until Lady Fanshaw had walked down the stairs and then she ran out to the mews.

'We shall do it, Edward!'

Edward was grooming one of the carriage horses.

'Do what, Abbie?'

'You shall become a harness-maker and I shall be a dressmaker. It's a dream come true!'

They were wed at the end of August and they moved into the rooms above the harness-maker's shop in East Smithfield.

It was a happy time and a busy one. Edward had much to learn about his new trade and Abbie found herself fully employed making dresses for Lady Fanshaw and her friends.

It was not possible to walk all the way to the West End, weighed down with materials, so Edward's uncle lent them a covered cart and a horse. Edward would drive the horse and Abbie would sit in the cart with her dresses and frills and flounces carefully laid out beside her.

They usually made at least one trip a week like this to the house in Cavendish Square or to other grand houses nearby. At Cavendish Square, the unpleasantness about Jim seemed to have blown over and Abbie was always welcomed by Mrs Plum and the other servants. Even Mrs Flanders seemed pleased to see her.

Then, one day, when they drew up at the back door, Mrs Plum came to greet them herself and her face was grave.

'I thought I should warn you, Abbie, dear, before you go inside.'

'Why? What's happened?'

Mrs Plum took her hand and helped her down from the cart.

'It's Sarah, Abbie. She's run away.'

'Oh no!'

Then, immediately. 'Not with . . . ?'

'Yes, I'm afraid she's run off with your brother. With Jim!'

Abbie looked horrified. 'Oh the silly girl. No good will come of it. He'll never make her happy.'

'I know, my dear, I know. But I'm afraid there's worse,' said Mrs Plum.

And, even before Mrs Plum said anything, a feeling of dread crept over Abbie, for she knew, with a ghastly certainly, what was coming.

'I'm afraid there are a lot of valuables missing from the house.'

'What sort of valuables?'

'Trinkets, mostly – snuffboxes, ornaments and the like. Oh, and some jewellery, too.'

'Oh no!' whispered Abbie.

'The police are out looking for Jim,' said Mrs Plum.

Abbie nodded silently. 'Thank you for telling me,' she said. She turned to Edward, who was still sitting up on the cart, his hands holding the reins.

'How will I tell Mam?' she asked him.

'Don't tell her, Abbie,' he advised. 'She's that weak, it would kill her.'

'But she'll find out.'

'How could she find out? She's too sick to walk up West now. Who would tell her?'

'Aye, you're right,' she said. Then, with a heavy heart, she unloaded her materials and walked into the house.

But the next time Abbie saw her, Mam guessed something was wrong. Frail though she was, and bent, despite not being an old woman by any means, she could still sense an atmosphere.

'Abbie, sommat's bothering you. What is it? Is it Jim?'

'No, Mam, I've not heard from Jim in months.'

Mam shook her head. 'Nor me; oh I hope he's not in trouble again, Abbie. Are you sure you know nothing?'

'No,' said Abbie, crossly. 'Nothing at all.'

'Well what is it girl, what's fretting you?'

Abbie hadn't meant to tell her yet, but suddenly she blurted it out. 'I'm having a baby, Mam. Come the spring you'll be a grandma!'

Mam's face lit up. 'Oh come here, my love,' she said, hugging her.

Abbie felt those familiar arms round her and started to cry. Her mam, who had been so strong, was as brittle as a bird.

Mam drew back. 'Just think,' she said. 'God willing, I shall be rocking your baby in my arms next springtime.'

But it was not to be. Mam died peacefully in her sleep just before Christmas. Abbie and Edward saw that she was decently buried in the churchyard along from her lodgings.

And Abbie's first child – a boy – was born the following spring.

6

Bedford, late August, present day

*I*t's ages since Katie and I went to London. The summer holidays are nearly over; and still nothing from Matt.

For the past few weeks, every day I've been watching the post like a hawk, but nothing.

In my letter, I'd told him everything I could think of. Everything that had happened since he left.

And now there's more to tell him.

I've had my first real boyfriend, for a start! Well, I've dumped him now, but we were quite an item, there, for a while.

And Katie's dyed her hair! Though I don't suppose that would interest Matt!

But what's most important is that Keith's gone! No surprise, really, but Mum finally made him go. The worm turned.

After I came back from London I had a real long chat with Mum, and I told her how I felt about Keith and how worried I was about her.

Although I didn't tell her about the London Connection, the visit has made me realise that perhaps I can change things here a bit — but letting her know how I feel.

I think it really shocked her. A few days after our talk, she signed on for this course. 'Empowerment' or some such rubbish.

Well, it certainly empowered Mum. Suddenly she started standing up to Keith and putting herself first.

And he didn't like it one bit!

So he's gone. And good riddance, so far as I'm concerned. He moved out last week and took all his stuff with him. Thank God they never actually got married. I hope she never takes up with another man or, if she does, I hope she has better taste next time.

And since he's gone, we get on a lot better. We talk about Matt again now Keith's not around, lurking in the corner like some moody dinosaur.

But I still haven't told her about my visit to the London Connection. I don't know why, really.

I just want to keep it to myself for a while. I think if Mum knew, she'd rush up there and start trying to find him again.

But she wouldn't find him, not unless he wanted to be found.

Somehow, I must find a way of letting him know that Keith's gone.

London, 1849

Abbie and Edward were very busy. Abbie had so much work as a dressmaker that she'd taken on a young girl to help her – and to help mind the two children, James and Victoria. James was six now, and little Victoria was three.

Edward worked hard, too, and had three young lads helping him. His uncle still lived with them, but he left Edward to run the business.

The rooms above the business had become too small for them and they had moved to bigger lodgings nearby where Abbie had room to spread out her materials and hang the finished garments. Edward had taught her how to drive the horse and cart; she was very nervous at first, but Edward had bought a docile cob to put between the shafts. The horse never shied or bolted and Abbie became very fond of him. And now she could take herself to her clients when Edward was too busy to come with her.

Abbie still did work for Lady Fanshaw and she'd even made the trousseau for Miss Eleanor's wedding.

But of Jim and Sarah there'd been no word.

Abbie often thought of them, though, and worried about them. She was glad she'd been able to spare her mam the news about the theft from Cavendish Square; at least she'd died thinking that Jim was an honest lad.

Most weeks, Abbie would visit Mam's grave. Sometimes she put a posy on it and often she found herself telling her mam about what had happened, how the children had done this and that.

Then one day in late summer, as she was kneeling by the grave, arranging a few flowers, a shadow fell across her. She'd not heard anyone coming and she looked round, startled.

A tall, shabbily dressed man stood looking down at her. His hair was matted and his eyes staring.

'Abbie?'

Abbie stood up, puzzled.

'Yes?'

'Abbie, don't yer know me?'

Abbie stepped back and her hand flew to her mouth. 'Jim!'

'Aye, it's me.'

She hadn't recognized him; he'd changed so much. He looked much older than his twenty-eight years. Some of his teeth were rotten and he smelt of strong drink.

'Oh Jim!' Abbie couldn't think what to say.

Jim passed his hand over his eyes. 'I come 'ere from time to time,' he said. He pointed at the flowers. 'I knew you tended the grave and I thought, one day, I might see yer 'ere.'

'How did you know she'd died?'

Jim looked down at his hands. 'I 'ear a lot, Abbie.'

'What are you doing, Jim? Where are you living? Is Sarah still with you?'

Jim frowned. 'Stupid chit! Yeah, she and the bairns are still hanging round me neck!'

'Bairns, Jim! You have children?'

Jim grunted. 'Twin boys,' he said shortly.

Abbie clapped her hands. 'What are their names, Jim? Come and sit over here and tell me about them – and about Sarah.'

She led him over to the churchyard wall and they sat side by side, in the sunshine.

'The boys are called Seth and Amos.'

'And what of Sarah?'

Jim didn't answer.

'Is she well?'

'Aye. Well enough.'

Abbie changed the subject. She could see that he wasn't going to talk much about Sarah.

'How are you living, Jim? Have you found work?'

Jim shrugged and looked away. 'This and that,' he said.

Abbie didn't press him further. She knew only too well what 'this and that' meant and she didn't want to hear; in any case, he wasn't likely to tell her the truth even if he gave her an answer.

'And does Sarah bring in any money?'

He shrugged again. 'She takes in laundry to wash, when she can, or does a bit of street collecting.'

Abbie, thinking of her own, comfortable life, felt guilty. Poor silly Sarah, losing her head over Jim and now driven to laundry work and picking up bits and pieces to sell from the streets.

'Bring her to see us, Jim, please,' she said.

Jim looked at her straight in the eye and, for a moment, she saw the old Jim, the brother she'd worshipped as he'd scuttled around the Whitechapel market selling apples to the toffs and their ladies.

'Abbie, you won't want nothing to do with the likes of us now,' he said. But he said it without rancour.

Abbie reached for his hand and held it tight. She noticed how his blackened fingernails contrasted with her own clean hands.

'You're my brother, Jim,' she said. 'Of course I want to see you – and Sarah, and the bairns.'

Jim shrugged. 'She's changed,' he said shortly.

'Even so,' persisted Abbie. 'I'd really like to see her. And to meet my little nephews, too.'

Jim looked at her. 'You sure, Abbie? You'll be shocked by 'ow she looks.'

'Of course I'm sure.'

'I'll send Sarah to see you, then,' he said, shortly, pulling his hand away from Abbie's.

Abbie looked stricken.

'Oh Jim! Can't I help you? Help you both?'

He shook his head, then got up to go.

'Wait, Jim, you don't even know where I live.'

He smiled then. 'Yeah, I do, Abbie. I've kept watch on yer, over the years. I know your nice lodgings along from the harness-maker's.'

'You've been there?'

'Only to catch a glimpse of you; to see you'd come to no 'arm.'

Abbie couldn't help herself then. She burst into tears.

Jim turned back suddenly and knelt down in front of her. He stroked her cheek.

'Don't take on so, Abbie. I can't bear to see you cry.'

Then he got up quickly and ran out of the churchyard.

But Abbie went on sitting on the churchyard wall in the sunshine, sobbing as if her heart would break.

That was the only time Jim had ever shown her any tenderness.

A few days later, on a sweltering September day, Abbie was driving the horse and cart back along her street when she noticed a wild-looking woman across the road from their lodgings.

She thought no more of it, reined up by the harness-maker's shop, and handed the horse and cart over to one of Edward's young apprentices. Then she walked the few hundred yards to her lodgings.

Just as she was opening the door, she felt a hand on her arm.

'Abbie?'

She turned round and frowned. Then she stared. It couldn't be – could it?

In front of her stood a scrawny, dirty woman with dull hair and a battered face. Her eyes were sunk deep in their sockets.

'Sarah?'

The woman nodded. 'Jim said to come and see you,' she whispered.

Abbie put her arm round Sarah's shoulders. She was shocked by how she looked. Much more shocked than she'd been by Jim's appearance.

'Come in, Sarah,' she said gently, leading her through the door.

Abbie's two children were home. They rushed to greet their mam and Abbie kissed them and then called for the girl who helped her.

'I saw a sherbert-seller coming down the road,' she said, fishing in her purse for a couple of pennies. 'Will you take the children and buy some – and for yourself, too.'

The children and the girl disappeared.

'Sit down, Sarah,' said Abbie, fetching a glass of water and handing it to her.

Sarah took the water and gulped it down thankfully.

'Oh Abbie,' she said at last. 'I'm that glad to see you.'

'And me you, Sarah,' said Abbie. 'But what's

happened to you? Where's that pretty cheeky chit of a girl I knew, with a ready smile and flashing eyes?'

Sarah looked down at the floor.

'You were right, Abbie,' she said.

'How was I right?'

'You said to me that Jim wouldn't make me happy.' Abbie took the glass from her.

'I know things are hard for you, Sarah. But I can help you both. I said that to Jim.'

Sarah shook her head. 'You don't know him, Abbie,' she whispered. 'He 'ates me and 'e's up to no good.'

Abbie sighed. 'You'd better tell me,' she said simply.

Sarah sniffed. 'I don't know where 'e gets 'is money and I don't ask, Abbie. All I know is 'e always 'as enough for the drink.' Her eyes met Abbie's for the first time. 'I dread it when 'e's bin drinking, Abbie.'

Abbie looked at Sarah's face. There was an old bruise on her cheek and a scar above her eye.

'Does he hit you, Sarah?'

Sarah nodded. 'Aye. 'E 'its me when 'e's bin drinking. Or if I ask for money and 'e don't feel like giving me none.'

'But the children?' said Abbie, her hand flying to the mouth. 'He doesn't hit them?'

Sarah shook her head. 'No, no, he's never beaten the children.'

Suddenly Abbie's mind went back to the description

Jim had given her of the beatings the children had taken at Point Puer.

'No,' she said slowly. 'I don't think he'd ever bring himself to beat a child.' Then she went on, 'Was it always like this, Sarah?'

Sarah sniffed again and wiped her nose with her hand. 'Oh no, when we were first together, it were grand. It were exciting then.'

'What did you do? How did you live?'

'He always seemed to 'ave money then. But I was a fool. I never knew where it had come from.'

'Did you know he'd stolen from Cavendish Square?'

Sarah hung her head. 'Only later,' she said, 'when I saw sommat I recognized. Sommat he couldn't sell, I suppose. But I never asked him about it. I didn't dare.' She gathered her shawl around her and shivered, despite the heat.

'How did he get into the house to steal it?'

Sarah hung her head.

'I let 'im in the night we ran away. 'E must 'ave took the stuff while I was getting ready.'

'Oh, Sarah!'

Sarah suddenly looked up. 'I 'ope it didn't cause trouble for you,' she said.

Abbie smiled. 'Of course it caused trouble for me, you silly goose, but it's all over now. That was a long time ago.'

'Oh Abbie, I'm sorry.'

'I was lucky, Sarah. Mrs Plum and Lady Fanshaw stood by me.'

Sarah nodded. 'They thought the world of you.'

Abbie continued. 'So, at first you were happy at least.'

'Oh yes. Stupid chit that I was; I thought 'e was wonderful. And life was so exciting after the washing and scrubbing and cleaning I'd been doing at Cavendish Square.'

'When did things start going wrong?'

'When I fell pregnant,' said Sarah simply.

'What happened?'

'I was that sick, Abbie. I didn't know what was 'appening to me, I was so stupid and ignorant, and Jim wanted me to be lively and that. He couldn't stand me being sick.'

'Poor Sarah. But was he pleased once the bairns were born?'

'Nah, not really. 'E's not one for taking on responsibility,' said Sarah bitterly.

They heard Abbie's two children coming back, laughing and calling out along the street outside.

'I'd best be going, Abbie,' said Sarah, biting her lip.

'Don't run away, Sarah,' said Abbie. 'Will you come again – next week – and bring the bairns with you? I so much want to see them. And bring Jim, too. I'm sure we can work something out for you all.'

'I don't think you can, Abbie,' said Sarah, lowering her voice.

'But why ever not?'

'Jim's in trouble, Abbie. 'E's on the run. They're after 'im.'

'Who?'

'The police. Things is getting too 'ot for 'im.'

Abbie stood up and put her hands on Sarah's shoulders. 'Please, Sarah. Tell him to come to us; whatever he's done, we'll try and help him.'

Sarah shook her head. 'You can't hide him from the law, can you?'

Abbie looked at her helplessly.

'You can't, Abbie. 'E's just got to keep running.'

'Well, give him the message. Promise me, Sarah.'

'Yes, I'll give it 'im. But it won't do no good.'

'And you'll come with the bairns to see us again?'

For the first time, Sarah smiled properly.

'I'd like that, Abbie,' she said. Then she sniffed again and went out of the door just as Abbie's two children were coming in.

Sarah walked quickly down the street, but she turned round once and stopped, looking at Abbie as she stood at her door, her arms round her children.

That night Abbie told Edward about Sarah's visit.

Edward rubbed his chin and stretched. 'I'd be happy to help her,' he said. 'I was always fond of Sarah.'

'But not of Jim?'

Edward shook his head. 'I'd help him if I could, Abbie, you know that, but 'e's that proud. I doubt 'e'd let us.'

Abbie hung her head. 'Sarah says he's in trouble. That the police are after him.'

Edward came up to Abbie and put his arm round her shoulders. 'We'll do what we can for them, I promise.'

Abbie turned and put her arms round his waist. 'You're a wonderful man, Edward, and I love yer.'

Edward grinned. 'I don't deserve you!'

A few days later, Abbie heard a soft knock on the door. She was alone, working on cutting out dress patterns, and her mouth was full of pins. Carefully, she removed them and set them on the table before going to answer the door.

Jim stood there, shuffling from one foot to the other.

'Quick, let me in, Abbie.'

Abbie drew him inside and shut the door.

'What is it, Jim?'

Jim went to the little window and stared out into the street.

'I think I've lost 'em,' he said. 'I wouldn't want them to come 'ere.'

'Lost who?'

'The damn bobbies,' said Jim.

Abbie looked at him for a long time. He returned

146

her stare and there was an understanding between them.

'You're in trouble, Jim, aren't you?'

Jim nodded, then he took a deep breath and sat down suddenly on the chair by Abbie's table. Absently, he picked up some pins and let them drop, one by one.

'They're on to me now, Abbie. And this time they've got evidence.'

Abbie said nothing.

'I'm going to have to disappear, Abbie. If I get caught this time it'll be Newgate and the hangman's noose, for sure.'

Abbie gasped and her hand felt for her own neck.

'What . . . what will you do?' she whispered.

Jim looked down at his blackened hands. 'I can get a passage on one of the ships sailing out to Australia,' he said.

'Australia! But you hated your time . . .'

'Aye. I hated Point Puer. But this time, I'd be free. I could maybe make a life for myself. There's gold to found there, Abbie. I'd go to work in the goldfields in Victoria.'

'But how? How would you get a passage if the bobbies are after you?'

Jim looked up. 'You remember I told you about the guard who was good to me when I went out to Point Puer?'

'Yes, you said he was the only one who treated you like a human being.'

Jim nodded. 'I never forgot him.'

'So? Have you seen him again?'

Jim nodded again. 'I met up with 'im a few days ago and we got talking. 'E knew what we went through at that hell-hole.'

Abbie kept quiet.

'Anyway, 'e's going out to Australia on one of the passenger ships and 'e says they need a few more hands and 'e can get me work on board.'

Abbie stared at him. 'Do you mean,' she said slowly, 'that you'd go on your own?'

Jim looked up at her. 'I couldn't take Sarah and the bairns,' he said. 'Anyways, Abbie, they're better off without me.'

'But Jim, she's your wife!'

He shook his head. 'Nah, we never bothered to get wed.'

'Well, she's your wife in all but name then; you can't abandon her!'

Jim stood up and came over to where Abbie stood, across the table from him, clasping and unclasping her hands.

'Honest, Abbie, I don't love her and she'd do better without me; you can see that!'

'Jim!'

'Please, Abbie, I'm begging you to see after her

when I'm gone. Her and the bairns.'

Abbie stood, white-faced, looking at him. He dug in the pockets of his coat and brought out two roughly wrapped packages.

'Look,' he said. 'I've scraped together all the money I can.' He handed one of the packages over to Abbie. 'Please, Abbie, please use it to help set her up. You can find her some decent lodgings and some honest work.'

Abbie stared down at the package in her hands. 'Where's this money come from, Jim?'

'I've earned it,' he said, suddenly flaring with anger. 'I've earned it with six years of hell being punished for sommat I never did.'

Abbie swallowed but didn't reply. When he flared with anger like that, she was scared of him.

'When will you go?' she asked.

'The ship sails tomorrow,' he said quietly. 'On the morning tide.'

'Oh Jim!' Abbie felt the tears coming to her eyes. She put the package down on the table and wiped her eyes, fiercely.

'I doubt I'll see you again, Abbie,' said Jim.

Abbie couldn't help the sobs escaping. 'Jim!'

His eyes had filled with tears, too. 'It's better this way,' he said gently.

'Perhaps,' she muttered. 'But Jim, maybe, one day . . .'

He shook his head. 'Only in the next life, Abbie,' he

said. Then he laughed. 'Though you'll be in 'eaven and I'll be in hell!'

She took his hand. 'You don't deserve to go to hell,' she said. 'You've been there already.'

He smiled and turned towards the door. 'Good luck, Abbie. And see after Sarah for me!'

'You will tell her, won't you?' said Abbie. 'Don't leave without telling her.'

He said nothing.

'*Please* tell her, Jim. For my sake'.

'Very well,' he mumbled. Then he handed her a second package.

'This is for you,' he said.

And then he was gone. He stumbled to the door and went out without a backward glance.

Abbie watched from the window as he ran down the street, dodging the horses and carts and the street sellers. When he had disappeared from view, she sat down at the table, put her head on her arms and sobbed as though her heart would break.

She was still there when Edward returned a little later. Slowly, haltingly, she told him what had happened.

'Maybe it is for the best, Abbie,' he said gently. 'He might make something of himself in Australia.'

'If the police don't get him.'

Edward shook his head. 'They'll forget 'im, once the trail's gone cold.'

'Poor Sarah,' sighed Abbie.

'Where is she?' asked Edward.

Abbie shook her head. 'I don't know where she is, but she'll come here, I'm sure, once he's gone.'

7

London, 1849

But it was another week before Sarah came to their lodgings.

She arrived with a pitifully small bundle of possessions slung on her back and leading two small boys, one by one hand and one by the other.

Abbie put her arms round her.

'Oh Sarah!' She couldn't think what else to say.

' 'E's gone, Abbie!'

Abbie frowned. 'Didn't he say anything?'

'The night before 'e left, he told me things were getting too hot for him. He said 'e'd have to disappear for a while and he told me to come 'ere.'

'Have the police been round?'

Sarah nodded. 'The bobbies 'ave been pestering me, asking me where 'e is. But I dunno, Abbie. I swear I dunno.'

Abbie looked at Sarah and the two little boys and her heart went out to her. Maybe Jim was right not to tell Sarah. Maybe she would have blurted it out to the bobbies.

'He came to see me, Sarah,' she said gently.

'Did he tell you where 'e's gone?'

Abbie nodded. 'He's gone back to Australia, Sarah. He left a week ago.'

Sarah sat down suddenly on the doorstep. She didn't say anything. One of the boys began bellowing.

Abbie bent down. 'Come inside,' she said. 'We'll look after you.'

London, 1850

Abbie's dressmaking business was thriving, but always, at the back of her mind, was the picture of her mam, her eyesight failing, squinting to mend and patch other people's linen.

'I'm only as good as my eyes, Edward,' she'd say, as he constantly told her how well she was doing.

So with great care she chose people to help her. She had two girls helping her now, clean, neat and keen to learn. Patiently, she'd teach them all she knew and gradually give them more responsibility. They were young and their eyes were bright.

And then there was Sarah.

Abbie sighed as she hung up another finished dress.

Sarah would never be a dressmaker, but she tried so hard.

She had changed. She had been beaten down by her time with Jim. She was pathetically grateful to Abbie and Edward for taking her in and setting her up with work.

They'd found her lodgings a few doors away and, at first, Abbie paid her for the stitching she did. But it soon became obvious that she wasn't worth the money, and she knew it.

'Abbie, you can't pay me for this,' she said one day, holding up a badly stitched hem.

'You'll get better,' said Abbie kindly.

But Sarah burst into tears. 'I won't, Abbie. I'm all fingers and thumbs. I can't do it. I'm no good at anything. I'm no use to you.'

Abbie thought fast.

'Sarah,' she said. 'Come here.' Sarah shuffled over to her, head downcast. Abbie put her arms round her.

'Sarah. I've bin thinking.'

Sarah said nothing.

'Could you take care of the bairns – all of them – for us?'

For a moment, Sarah's face brightened, but then she said, looking fearfully into the next room. 'But that's Edna's job.' Abbie followed her gaze and watched Edna trying to amuse all four children.

'Please, Sarah, it would be much better.' Abbie

squeezed her hand. 'Edna's going to be a good dressmaker one day. She's handy with her needle and quick to learn. And she's not so good with the children as you are.'

'But you can't pay me to mind the bairns, Abbie!'

'I certainly can,' said Abbie. 'Remember Cavendish Square. You can be a nursery maid!'

'My,' said Sarah, giggling with some of her old spirit. 'A nursery maid!'

'Yes,' said Abbie, grinning. 'A nursery maid for the under housemaid!'

Then, suddenly, they both fell to laughing at the situation.

But soon Sarah stopped. 'I'll do it for free, Abbie. It's the least I can do. I've been living off you for the past few months, you feeding me and finding me lodgings and clothes and that – and the twins, too. It's not as if Jim gave you any money, either, the mean sod.'

Abbie stood still. She had put to the back of her mind the package that Jim had given her. In the end, she and Edward hadn't opened either of the packages. They'd decided to help Sarah and the twins on their own and not use what they were sure was stolen money.

'He did give me something for you, Sarah,' said Abbie, slowly. 'I'm sorry. I should have handed it to you right away but . . .'

'But you knew it was stolen money?'

Abbie nodded. 'I didn't like to . . .'

Sarah sighed. 'You were right,' she said at last.

Abbie went to the other side of the room and rummaged in her bureau. It had been a present from Edward and had been made by one of his cabinet-maker friends who had fallen on hard times. It was here that she kept all the papers about her business and anything else of importance.

She took a key from a string sewn at her waist and unlocked one of the drawers. With a heavy heart, she took out the two packages which Jim had handed to her just before he left.

She walked back across the room with them.

'This one is for you,' she said. 'And the other one he said was for me.'

Sarah took the package and let it fall into her lap.

Abbie fetched some scissors and then knelt down beside Sarah and patted her hand.

'Come on, Sarah,' she said, 'we'll open them together.'

She cut the string on her own and unwrapped the layers of stained paper. She already had an idea what was inside, but, even so, her heart beat faster and she glanced furtively around when it lay in her hands.

She held it up. A finely wrought gold snuffbox, with a beautiful enamelled picture of bejewelled ladies on the lid and an inscription on the bottom.

Slowly, she traced the words with her finger. 'Presented to the Honorable Percy Fanshaw by his fellow officers.'

Sarah was staring at it, too.

'You'd best put it away, Abbie,' she said.

Abbie nodded and began wrapping up the little box again and retying the string around the package.

Meanwhile, Sarah had opened her package. Her eyes widened.

'Abbie, there's a lot of money 'ere. Fifty pounds or more! What shall I do?'

For a moment, Abbie hesitated, then she remembered those bitter words of Jim's: 'I've earned it. I've earned it with six years of hell, being punished for summat I never did.'

'Keep it, Sarah,' said Abbie quietly. 'There may come a time when the boys need it. Keep it.'

Sarah wrapped it up again and handed it back to Abbie.

'Put it back in the desk then, Abbie,' she said. 'It'll be our secret.'

Abbie rose and took it from her. 'They'll both be our secret, Sarah,' she said, then she put the packages back in the bureau drawer and locked it.

And for years, neither of them ever mentioned Jim's packages.

Bedford, October, present day

It's happened! I can't believe it! He's been in touch!

Today was just an ordinary day; well, p'raps not that ordinary. Mum's finally decided to move house. I think it's a great idea. There are too many memories here. Of Dad and of Keith – and of Matt, of course.

But she keeps saying what if Matt decides to come back here? And I keep telling her that someone would tell him where we'd gone. We don't mean to go far. Just a mile or two away. I'll still be able to go to the same school.

But it will be a new start.

Anyway, we'd been talking about this for ages and then, this morning, at breakfast, Mum suddenly said she'd definitely decided we would move. That she'd go to the estate agent today and arrange to put the house on the market.

She seemed really excited about it. I've not seen her look so bright for ages. I gave her a big hug.

Anyway, I was just leaving for school when I saw the postman draw up outside our house. I met him at the gate and took the mail from him. There were the usual circulars, a few boring envelopes for Mum and a bulky one for me.

I slipped the others back through the letterbox and put the bulky one in my schoolbag. Then I ran down the road – late, as usual.

I got so caught up with things at school that it wasn't until break that I looked at the letter. The address was typewritten, on a label.

I thought it was probably something I'd ordered over the net, then forgotten about. Casually, I undid the envelope.

It was a CD.

I turned it over, frowning. I thought there must be some mistake. It wasn't something I'd ordered.

I looked at the title and the picture on the front. The group was called Jacob's Footstool and there was a picture of four blokes lounging about at a railway station. I looked carefully at the faces, still frowning. And then, suddenly, as I stared at one of the faces, I screamed out loud, 'MATT!'.

Katie had been talking with some other girls. She rushed over when I screamed. But by this time I'd opened the CD and looked at the names inside.

And there it was; as large as life, on the credits: MATTHEW FORD, LYRICS AND KEYBOARD.

Well, you can imagine the scene. I was laughing and crying, Katie was shaking me, trying to get me to say what had happened, and our form mistress was beside me, trying to calm me down.

At last, when I'd managed to explain, someone found a CD-player and we all listened.

And BOY was it GOOD! I couldn't stop crying. Listening to the music brought it all back. And even I could hear how he'd come on. He must have been working at his music all this time, ever since he left. There was so much I wanted to know. How had he got the CD made? Who were the others?

I didn't do much work for the rest of the day. I was longing to get home and play it to Mum. I didn't phone her. I wanted *it to be a surprise.*

But it was Katie who had the best idea. I let her look at the cover and, when she turned it over, she said quietly, 'Becky, there's an email address here.'

I snatched it back from her then and I was all for rushing off to the school computer, but she stopped me.

She was right, of course. He's sure to get it, if I send an email to the band's address, and I need to think carefully what to say.

The next day . . .
I've sent it, at last.

Mum's been in such a state since we got the CD. She's been playing it over and over and, every time she does, she starts to cry.

It took a long time to work out what to say, but in the end, we sent a joint email to the band's address. We told Matt that we're going to move house. We told him that Keith had gone out of our lives for ever and that he'd left the area to take a job up in the north.

I was surprised at Mum. I thought she'd be all emotional and sloppy, but she wasn't. She said how impressed she'd been by the CD, what a professional job they'd made of it, how we longed to see Matt but that she'd never expect him to come back to live at home if he didn't want to. It was only at the end that she said how much she loved him and how much she missed him.

Two days later . . .

Between us, Mum and I must have checked the emails just about every ten minutes for the last two days, but there's been no reply. We were both getting quite scratchy and bad-tempered with the strain of waiting.

Then, this afternoon, as I was walking back from school, talking to a friend on my mobile, I was suddenly conscious of someone following me. You know how it is: you get that feeling, even if you can't hear footsteps.

I whipped round, scared.

And for a moment, I stayed scared. There was a man behind me, half hidden by the end of a building. Then the man stepped out on to the pavement.

'Becky.'

Until he spoke, I didn't recognize him. He'd grown and filled out. He wasn't a boy any longer.

I stared at him. It was Matt all right, but there were lines on his face and his eyes seemed darker, somehow.

And then he smiled, the smile I remembered, and I dropped my phone and my school bag and ran to him.

London, January 1850

Sometimes, when the children were asleep and Edward was dozing by the fire after a hard day's work, Abbie would slip out and go round to Sarah's lodgings.

The rooms were small, but light and airy. Sarah

would never be tidy, like Abbie, but she kept the place clean and Abbie always enjoyed visiting her there.

One evening, when she was visiting, they got to talking about the old times at Cavendish Square.

'It were 'ard,' said Sarah, 'but it were fair.'

Abbie nodded. 'Like my mam said, you had food and shelter regular and that's a lot when you've had to live like we did.'

Sarah agreed. 'Jim used to tell me about the times when you worked in the market, the two of you. It must have bin rough.'

Abbie shrugged. 'We were young; and we didn't know aught else, Sarah. If it hadn't bin for my mam making me learn my letters and watching over me when I sewed my first seam, I might have ended up there running a stall in all weathers, like old Lil.'

'Or collecting rags and metal from the streets, like I did,' murmured Sarah.

'Oh, I'm sorry, I didn't mean . . .'

Sarah smiled and changed the subject. 'And what of your own bairns, Abbie? They'll not 'ave to work on the market will they, or serve as a maid in a grand house?'

Abbie sat back in her chair. 'I dunno, Sarah. They're that young, we've not thought of it, but maybe one day they'd take on what we're doing – the harness-making and dressmaking.'

Sarah sighed. 'I wonder about mine, too. Seth's a

steady lad, but my Amos!'

Abbie laughed. 'He's a little tearaway, your Amos.'

'I don't see how they can be twins, they're so different,' said Sarah. 'When Seth plays with sommat, Amos snatches it away.'

'And Seth's so good. He doesn't fight back.'

'Maybe 'e should,' said Sarah. 'Amos gets 'is way too often.'

She looked at Abbie. ' 'E worships Edward. I think 'e misses his dad.'

'Jim was good to them, wasn't he?' said Abbie.

Sarah shrugged. 'In 'is own way, I think 'e loved them.'

'Maybe, one day, he'll see them again,' said Abbie.

Sarah shook her head. 'If he's got any sense he'll stay out in Australia.'

'I wonder if he's found any gold? Mebbe he'll make 'is fortune!'

' 'Ere, Abbie, I'm the dreamer, not you!'

They both laughed, then Amos woke up and demanded his mother's attention.

Abbie looked on as Sarah tried to reason with him. At eight years old, Amos was the spitting image of his father. And he had the same cheeky smile. With Amos it was either all sunshine or all storm. His tantrums were wild and he'd throw things around, but then when he smiled, the sun came out and your heart melted.

Between them, they settled him at last. Sarah sat beside him until he fell asleep, his thumb in his mouth, while Abbie looked on, thinking of what she was doing at his age. When she was eight, she was already making herself useful on the market, earning a penny here and there to take home to Mam and Pa. She was often barefoot and her clothes were ragged and patched, even when Mam mended them.

The life for her children, and for Sarah's children, would be easier than that. They'd learn about hard work, to be sure, but, God willing, if she and Edward worked hard, they'd never go hungry.

London, June 1850

The months went by and gradually Abbie and Sarah talked less and less about Jim. Then, one day, Abbie returned home at dinner time, expecting to find Sarah there, with little Victoria, waiting for the boys to come back from the dame school a few streets away where they spent most mornings.

She walked in through the door and was surprised to see a man sitting there, in silence, while Sarah sat opposite him, with Victoria clinging to her knee.

Sarah looked scared and got up immediately and came over to Abbie. 'Oh Abbie, I'm that glad you've come 'ome,' she whispered.

Abbie looked at the man. She could see immediately that he was a sailor. Her heart started beating very fast and the colour rose to her cheeks. Had he come with news of Jim?

' 'E says he must speak to you, Abbie,' said Sarah, twisting her hands together nervously.

Slowly, Abbie removed her bonnet and patted her hair. She picked up Victoria and kissed her.

'Have you offered the gentleman something to drink, Sarah?'

The man cleared his throat. 'I'll not stay long,' he mumbled.

Abbie took a deep breath. 'You've come with news of Jim, haven't you?' she said.

He nodded and looked at Sarah.

'She says she's his wife?' he said.

Abbie nodded. 'She is,' said Abbie firmly.

'He never mentioned a wife,' said the sailor, looking uncomfortable, 'just his sister.'

Sarah looked down at the floor.

'What is your news?' asked Abbie, quietly. 'Whatever it is, his wife has a right to know.'

The man shuffled uncomfortably in his seat.

'I was a guard on the ship that took him out to Point Puer when he was a lad,' he said.

Abbie relaxed. 'He told me about you,' she said quietly. 'He said you were the only one who treated him like a human being.'

The man looked up. 'That hell-hole,' he said quietly. 'If a lad went there with any goodness in him, that place soon knocked it out of him.'

'And you got him the passage back, I believe?'

The man nodded again. 'I feel bad about it now,' he said at last. 'At the time I thought I was doing 'im a favour.'

Abbie's throat was dry. She swallowed. 'So, sir, do you have news of my brother?'

The sailor ran his hand through his shaggy crop of hair. 'Not exactly, ma'am.'

'Please tell us what you know,' said Sarah, finding her voice at last.

The man got up from his chair. 'Well, I went out on the ship with him,' he said. Then he hesitated.

'Please, please tell us what you know,' said Abbie, losing patience. She set Victoria down and went over to Sarah and held her hand.

'The ship was wrecked,' he said simply. 'Wrecked off that wicked east coast of Victoria. It's that bad they call it the shipwreck coast.'

'But you survived!' said Abbie.

He nodded.

'And Jim?' whispered Sarah.

The man looked at her then.

'I'm sorry, ma'am. I was one of the lucky ones.'

Abbie squeezed Sarah's hand hard.

'Did they ever find his body?' blurted out Sarah.

The man shook his head. 'Washed away,' he said, 'like most of the poor souls.'

'But they never found it.'

'No.'

'Could he have escaped? Might he have run away?'

The sailor looked at the floor. 'No, ma'am, the coast there is treacherous. High sharp cliffs right down to the sea and terrible big waves.'

'But you survived!'

'Aye. A few of us got into a rowing boat. But it was touch and go. The waves pounded us and three of our number died anyway. Then we were thrown on to the rocks. We would have drowned soon enough, but we'd been seen and some brave local men risked everything to save us.'

'So you're sure he's drowned?' said Abbie, slowly, still holding Sarah's hand.

'Certain, ma'am. He couldn't have survived.'

Bedford, November, present day

Matt didn't stay long, that first time. Mum and I tried not to ask too many questions, not to probe.

His life has changed so much. He's looked after himself for too long to come home. But he's doing OK. He's nearly finished school and he's got a place at college to learn about music therapy. He knows where he's going and he'll get there, I know he will.

But he'll never settle back to life in Bedford. Why should he?

At least we know where he is and we know he's well — and safe.

The relief is written all over Mum's face. She smiles all the time and hums around the house, just like she did before Keith came on the scene.

Three months later . . .

We're moving house at last! Mum's found a really great house not far from here but it's nearer the town centre so I can get to the shops and the clubs without too much hassle — and Mum can get into work, too. She's starting a new job soon. She's quite scared about it, but I keep telling her she'll be great.

So we've been packing up and sorting out and throwing away. You would not believe all the junk I found.

Sometimes I've caught Mum standing, staring into space. Usually when she's holding something of Dad's, or Matt's. Keith took everything with him so at least we don't have to clear out any of his stuff.

We started on the attic today. It took for ever. We kept stopping and looking at old photos and giggling at me and Matt as babies and Mum and Dad when they were going out together.

Then we came across a big box I'd never seen before. I

asked Mum what it was and she couldn't remember, so we opened it up.

It turned out it was a whole lot of stuff from Gran (Mum's mum) and from Gran's mum, too. There were some really funny photos; the things they wore then were unbelievable. There were a few books, too, and a big Bible.

Mum said she remembered Gran giving her the box but she'd forgotten what was inside.

Then Mum went downstairs and I stayed up in the attic, having a good rummage. There wasn't much of value in the box – just family mementoes, I suppose, but at the bottom there were a couple of packages, all tied up with string.

Well, I'd got this far, so I thought I might as well take a look inside them. I started on the first one. The string was rotten and it broke off easily. Then I got to unwrapping all the layers of paper. It was all stiff and some of it disintegrated in my hands.

Then, inside, there was a whole lot more wrapping, but this time it was cloth.

I unwound the cloth and something dropped into my lap.

It was an old-fashioned gold watch with a heavy chain and on the back of the watch there was some writing: 'To my son, Charles Frobisher, on the occasion of his marriage. From his father. June 1830.'

I was riveted. Quickly, I undid the second package.

This time, I found a little gold snuffbox with a picture on the top. Even I could tell that the watch and the snuffbox were old – and probably valuable. I turned the snuffbox over, and there was some writing on the bottom of that, too: 'Presented to the Honorable Percy Fanshaw by his fellow officers.'

I sat up there in the attic, looking at the two pieces.

I wonder where they came from?

Who were these people – Charles Frobisher and Percy Fanshaw?

And what on earth did they have to do with Gran – or Great-Gran?